RUINS OF EMBER

MELANIE TAYS

Copyright © 2020 by Melanie Tays

MelanieTays.com

All rights reserved. This book or any portion thereof may not be reproduced or used in any manner whatsoever without express written permission, except for the use of brief quotations in a book review.

Published by Goldlight Enterprises LLC
Published in Queen Creek, Arizona, USA

ISBN: 978-1-952141-05-8 (paperback)
ISBN: 978-1-952141-04-1 (ebook)

CHAPTER 1

Waves of heat radiate from the blazing inferno behind us—the wall of fire that has just been lit to keep the five of us from ever coming near The City again. The air is so hot it's painful just to breathe. The sky is dark, the fire our only source of light. Together we flee, running as fast as our legs can carry us, fueled by adrenaline and a desperate desire to survive.

But even as we escape the danger at our backs, the roaring sound of an airplane's engine announces that we're not alone out here. I don't know who's on that plane or why they've been bombing The City—or attempting to, at least—for the past few days. I have no way of knowing if they're here to help us or inflict new tortures, and I'm not ready to find out.

I'm the fastest runner among us—even with my injured leg, festering with infection—and I lead us toward a small cave carved into an enormous rock. It's only another fifty yards away. If we hurry, we can probably make it before we're spotted by the airplane, and we should be safe from the fire there, too.

There's an ear-piercing scream, and I turn back to see Kamella's head encompassed in angry, biting flames.

Vander is at her side, and he throws her to the ground, using the dirt to smother her hair and sustaining burns of his own in the process.

"Get in the cave," I yell to Ty as I sprint back for the others. I want us all out of sight as soon as possible. Once there, we can rest and figure out what our next move should be.

Shawny hobbles along, barely outpacing the fire that bounds from tree to tree as though stalking us.

"Keep moving!" I command. "You're almost past the trees."

Kamella tries to stand, but before she can, Vander picks her up, slings her over his shoulder, and takes off running.

"This way," I yell to be heard over the crackling of the fire. I lead them back toward the cave where Ty stands waving to us.

Shawny reaches us moments later and collapses to the cold stone ground, clutching her hugely pregnant belly.

When we're all inside, I heave a sigh of relief and stand at the entrance looking out, assessing our situation. I'm counting on the open, barren dirt surrounding the cave's entrance to protect us from the fire, but it turns out to be unnecessary. In astonishment, I watch as the fire, unnaturally ignited by a thick fog, holds its position twenty feet away, not spreading to the other trees easily within its reach. However this is possible, it explains the stark contrast between the lush forest and the ashen plain surrounding The City's border—or what was The City's outer border until moments ago, when the barrier field shifted to swallow the Ash and expel the five of us.

Even though the night sky is black, I shield my eyes against the brightness of the menacing flames. The airplane has passed over, seemingly unaware of our presence. It hovers over The City, dropping what appears in the distance to be small, black balls. A few pass straight through the barrier field; most of them are repelled and bounce and roll off to be consumed in the fire.

I place a hand on my chest to calm my racing heart, and I inhale deeply. For the moment, we're safe. We can stay here tonight, giving sleep a chance to help us make sense of all that just happened. In the morning, we can decide what to do next.

I hear the plane circle around and come back toward us, but there's no way they'll spot us tucked away in the crevice of this rock under the cover of darkness.

Suddenly, an agonizing scream slices through the night air, rising above the roar of the airplane and the crackling flames. I turn to find Shawny writhing on the ground, breathing hard and clutching her stomach. I drop to her side and reach for her hand. Her skin is cold and damp. I don't know much about these things, but something must be terribly wrong.

"Can you sit up?" I ask, for some reason believing if she can at least just pull herself upright then she'll recover.

She makes a weak effort, and then cries out and collapses back.

"No, don't move," Kamella says, dropping to her

knees and gently touching Shawny's stomach. I don't know what she's doing, but whatever it is, her actions appear purposeful. "She needs help," Kamella proclaims, "or she's going to lose the baby."

Another scream reverberates off of the cave walls, half-physical and half-mental anguish.

I look around for anything that can help us, but there's nothing here. And though Kamella seems to know a thing or two about how to care for injured people, I highly doubt she knows how to deliver a baby under these circumstances. Besides, Kamella looks like she should be the one writhing in pain right now, with her hair scorched and her face and neck splotched with red and purple blisters.

Ty takes a seat by the wall, looking bewildered but not truly concerned. He won't be any help. He wouldn't even be here if I hadn't held onto him as the barrier shifted and expelled the rest of us who had received the Mind Mist antidote. I'm not sure I did him a favor by bringing him along, since he's still under the influence of the Mind Mist.

"What do we do?" Vander asks, frantic. After spending days with Vander in the Ash, I know he's tough, but he's also the one who passed out when it was time to cauterize the wound on my leg. I don't think he's up for a challenge like this. He's also holding his hands out gingerly, and I can tell he's trying to not to exacerbate his painfully burned palms.

No amount of sleep and perspective is going to fix this

by morning. In fact, by morning one or more of us may be dead. There's only one possible hope I can see, and I don't give myself time to debate it for fear I'll lose my nerve.

"Ty, come with me," I yell, and I take off running out of the cave.

Ty follows without question or argument.

The airplane is still overhead, but moving fast. I wave my arms frantically in the air and instruct Ty to do the same. He really gets into this, as though this is all a fun game. But the plane keeps moving, passing over and flying away.

"No," I scream, and take off running after it.

In order to follow the airplane, we're forced to travel up a steep incline. Every step sends a jolt of pain through my injured leg, but I refuse to let that slow me.

We holler and jump and wave our arms around like crazed animals until the airplane has flown so far ahead of us that there's no hope they'll see or hear us, and we finally stop.

I collapse to the ground, my leg cramping and seething with pain, my throat dry and sore from screaming.

Ty takes a seat next to me. "I guess they didn't hear us."

I don't respond. My head rests on the cool dirt, and I'm too stunned and tired and terrified to cry, so I just lay there. Soon, I'll have enough strength to walk again. Soon, I'll follow the orange glow back down this hill to the cave where Vander, Kamella, and Shawny are waiting for me to bring help—help that isn't coming. But right now, I just lay there trying to remember how to breathe.

"Oh, I guess they heard us," says Ty.

I sit up and turn my gaze to the sky, but the tiny lights of the plane are far in the distance now, the sound receding. "What do you mean?" I ask. "The airplane is still flying away."

"Not the airplane," Ty says, pointing behind me. "Him."

Startled, I turn and find myself face-to-face with the most hideous creature imaginable. Half-human, half-beast, it stares at me with deeply sunken eyes too aware to be animal, but its form is too mangled to be a human. It wears a soiled robe that doesn't hide the way its flesh droops from its bones, as though it's wearing the skin of something two or three times its size. Long, stringy, white hair hangs in thin, uneven patches from the top of its head. I can't even venture a guess at its gender or age.

This is a Roamer—a horrid, deteriorating, deadly survivor of the Withers plague. I'm sure of it. What else could it be? This is the very definition of terror that made the threat of being sent to the Ash a fate worse than death.

For a moment we just stare at each other, neither daring to move. Its expression is impossible to read. Slowly, I slide my legs up under me and get to my feet, careful not to startle it.

Suddenly the silence is broken, and I jump with a start.

"I'm Ty, what's your name?"

The Roamer's head snaps from me to Ty and it opens its mouth, its lips enormous and flopping wildly, revealing a toothless jaw. At least it can't bite us. It looks like maybe it's trying to speak, but all that comes out are incomprehensible growls and groans.

"Ty, get behind me," I whisper, feeling the need to protect him. It's my fault he's out here.

"Okay," Ty says with a shrug, and moves into my shadow.

The Roamer grunts again, a low, gurgling sound, and points off in the opposite direction from where we came.

"We're going to leave now," I say in a slow, measured tone.

When the Roamer doesn't react, I reach behind me, grip Ty's hand, and take a few slow steps sideways, moving away without turning my back on the creature.

This seems to agitate it, and it lunges for me. Grunting and growling, it latches onto my arm. I try to fight it off, but it's stronger than it looks, and it knocks me to the ground. My head smacks hard against a jagged rock, and my vision goes black for a moment. My ears start to ring, and the sound grows louder with every passing moment.

"Ty, help!" I yell.

"Here," he says, holding out a handful of flowers to the Roamer. He's clearly not going to be any help. It will be up to me to get us out of this.

The withered creature ignores him and grapples to keep me down and get a grasp on me. I twist and catch sight of a second, equally gruesome Roamer crouching just behind a nearby boulder.

"Run!" I yell to Ty. I may not be able to fight them off, but at least I can save one of us. "Just run!"

And he takes off back down the hill.

My head pounds, and warm blood runs down the side of my face. The Roamer has me by my injured leg and is dragging me off the way it was pointing before. I scream and kick it with my free leg, but my foot connects with nothing but flabs of skin and has no effect on the Roamer.

The second Roamer ambles forward and takes hold of my other leg, effectively cutting off any possible chance I had of breaking free.

I fight the impulse to cry out, to yell and beg for Vander to come save me. It would only put him and all the others in more danger, so I bite my tongue and do my best to fight against these demons alone.

They drag me farther away, turning behind a large rock and moving toward the black, ominous mouth of the hidden cave. I try not to imagine what they'll do to me once we're inside.

Even though I'm held fast, I twist and writhe to get free, but the pain in my injured leg is so intense that my brain threatens to pass out. I fight for consciousness and control. I remind myself that I've lived through worse than this.

My head rolls back and I see a trail of my own blood streaked across the dirt and rock. I hope Vander and the others don't see it and try to find me. As soon as Shawny has recovered, I hope they get as far away from here as possible.

I have no strength left to fight, and it hurts too much to try. I go limp and surrender to my fate. I lose sight of the glow that surrounds The City and am about to be forever lost to the abyss of the Roamers' cave when, suddenly, I see people descending from the sky, drifting down like feathers and landing all around me. I can't make sense of floating people, and I wonder if I'm already unconscious and dreaming.

Or maybe I'm already dead.

CHAPTER 2

Three people wearing thick black masks close in on the Roamers holding me. They point blasters, and my captors scurry away. Shrill screams slice through the night air, exacerbating the ringing and throbbing in my head. I search for the source of it, wishing it would stop.

"You're going to be all right," one of the men who just descended from the sky tells me, his voice muffled through the thick layers of his mask.

It's then that I realize the shrieks emanate from my own mouth. I clamp my jaw shut, and the sound and consequent pain are cut off.

The man stays with me, protecting me from the Roamers while the other two men run into the cave. Slowly, the Roamers slink away into the shadows and disappear.

The airplane we saw earlier now hovers overhead, and I realize that the growing noise wasn't just in my head. I wonder why the plane returned. Did someone on board see us after all?

"Who are you?" I stammer.

"I'm General Rockshire. We're with the SDRT."

"The what?"

But before he can answer, the others return from the cave, and they're carrying a small child—a boy, no older than five or six, with messy blond hair and dirt streaking his face and clothes. He appears perfectly normal except for the way his features contort in terror, and I wonder how he got there. He's too young to have been sent to the Ash from The City. Besides, until today the Ash was still inside the barrier field. No, he can't be from The City. So where did he come from?

"Are there more of you?" the man asks.

I hesitate. Even though I was chasing these people down not long ago, it still feels unnatural and risky to trust them. I have no idea who they are or what they intend to do with us. "It's okay," the man holding the child assures me. "We're here to help."

My mind reels, trying to process everything. "A doctor," I finally stammer.

"Yes, we'll get you to a doctor," General Rockshire promises.

"No, not me. Shawny. Her baby... She's pregnant," I say. "She needs a doctor."

"Where are the others?"

"In the cave at the base of the hill," I say, desperate to believe these people truly are here to help us. They did just save me and this little boy from Roamers. And what other choice do we have? None that I can see as I lie here on the ground, bruised and bleeding and just so tired.

"All right, we're going to get you two on board the

hoverplane," the general says. "Then we'll find your friends."

Before I can protest—insist they find the others and help them first—the men have slipped golden bands around my wrists and ankles.

"Here we go," one of them says.

Startled, I begin to rise into the air, lifted by the bands on all four limbs, pulled gently toward the aircraft above. The bands do their job well, lifting me steadily upward, but watching the ground fall away below is still a terrifying sensation.

As I'm drawn closer to the massive flying vehicle, I can see blades spinning on its underbelly covered by circular grating. It's so much bigger and more complex than the Wright brothers' plane from the history books. That machine only held a few passengers, while this is more like a hovering building that could carry hundreds. A door on the side of the plane slides open as I near, and the golden bands deposit me on the floor inside. The space is small and well lit, with yellow, metal walls. There's another closed door across the room with a large glass window through which a woman with short, black hair wearing a white coat stands watching me.

Moments later one of the rescuers floats into the room, holding the frightened boy. He sets him down and leaps back out into the open sky.

I gasp and crawl to the open door to peer out after him. But he descends gently all the way back to the ground. It wasn't just in my imagination. These people really can fly—and not just in an airplane or hoverplane. Even if it's only because of these bracelets, it's no less miraculous. How I wish Whyle could see this. It's even better than the stories Dad tells.

"Back away from the door," a woman's voice instructs. I scoot back and turn to the woman on the other side of the glass. "Good, now prepare for decontamination," she says, her voice unnaturally carried and amplified through the room.

The door slides shut, and a red gas begins to fill the room. Instinctively, I cover my mouth and nose to avoid breathing it in.

"Don't fight it," she says. "It won't hurt you. It will decontaminate your body, inside and out. It's important to breathe normally and let it do its job."

For the first time in all the confusion and terror of the night, I realize I've just been exposed to the Withers. That I could get sick and turn into one of those hideous creatures—if I don't die an agonizing death first. This red gas must be meant to protect me from that fate. With that in mind, I inhale deeply, willing it to permeate every cell in my body.

The child, who had been standing rigid just where he was left, begins to cry and runs to the door, clawing for a way out. The woman watching from the other side of the door is unmoved by his pleas.

"It'll be okay," I try to reassure him, even though I'm not entirely sure of this fact myself. But it doesn't matter, because my words have no effect on him. I try to stand, but my legs won't support me. I yelp in pain, and the boy turns his fearful brown eyes on me as though I might attack him.

"It's okay," I repeat, holding my hands and arms out to show him I'm not a threat.

He stops crying and appraises me for a long moment. I'm not sure what he's looking for as he stares into my face. But suddenly he smiles and runs to me, nestling in the space between my open arms. It's not exactly what I was expecting, but I wrap my arms around the boy and hold onto him as though he were my own precious little brother.

Finally, the air clears. Then the door separating us from the watching woman opens, and she walks toward us as the door slides closed behind her.

"Welcome," says the woman with a warm smile. "My name is Doctor Gill. You're safe here."

I don't bother to point out that I was assured for my entire life that inside the Safe Dome was the safest place possible, and that turned out to be an insane lie. Promises of safety don't carry a lot of weight for me at the moment. I pull the boy, whose arms still cling to my neck, tighter to me.

Again the door opens, and a man rushes in. He's several inches shorter than me, with light brown hair and a stubbly face, as though he's forgotten to shave for the past several days.

"What are you doing here?" Doctor Gill asks, clearly not pleased to see him.

"They're the first out of Ten. I need to talk to them," the man insists, looking at me and the boy as though we're some kind of present sent here just for him.

He steps toward us, and Doctor Gill places a hand on his chest to stop him. "Later," she insists. "Can't you see they need help?"

"I heard there were more," he says. "Are there more of you?"

I've already told the men on the ground about the others, and I'm sure they'll be here soon, so trying to keep it a secret now won't do any good, no matter how uncomfortable this man's gaze is making me.

"There are four others," I say. "They need help, too."

"We're going to help all of you," Doctor Gill assures me.

The man ignores her. "I'm Commander Elben. I'm in charge of the SDRT."

"The SD…what?"

"SDRT: Safe Dome Recovery Team," he says. "It's essential that you tell me everything that has happened."

"Later, Maxton," Doctor Gill says, her manner stern. I get the feeling that few people ever stand up to Commander Elben, and he doesn't like it.

"Fine, you're the doctor," he says with mock deference. "But I want them all in the conference room first thing in the morning," he says, and storms out. On his way out the door, he passes a girl pushing a narrow, rolling bed.

"Tella, what took you so long?" Doctor Gill asks.

"We've got to get them out of here so we can bring the next group up."

My ears perk up at this. So they've found them? "Are the others okay?" I ask.

"We'll know soon enough," says Doctor Gill. "Let's get you up on the stretcher and take you to the Hospital Wing."

I try to let go of the boy, but he won't have it. I manage to disentangle his arms from around my neck and take his hand instead. With Tella's help, I stand, wincing and biting my lower lip so I don't scream in pain. My head spins, but soon I'm sitting on the stretcher, the boy next to me, and we're being rolled out of the room.

"What's your name?" I say to the boy, but he doesn't answer. "My name is Emery," I say.

"That's a nice name," says Tella.

"Thanks," I mutter, even though it's the boy from whom I'm trying to elicit a response. "Where did you come from?" I try again.

He turns to me and grunts, the sound so similar to the grotesque sounds made by the Roamers that I almost jerk away.

"He probably can't talk," Tella says.

"What?" I ask. "How do you know?"

"None of the children of the Withered can. At least, nothing more than grunts and groans."

"Children of the Withered? You mean those Roamers are this boy's parents?" I ask in disbelief.

"Yes, the people who survived the Withers can

sometimes still have children, who all seem to be immune to the disease. But since the effects of the Withers results in a loss of the ability to speak, they can't teach their kids to speak."

I gaze at the child, stunned. He looks nothing at all like those barely-human creatures that attacked me. But if they're his parents, then this boy's fear is not of them, but of the people who just came into his home and ripped him away from his family.

"But the Roamers—or Withered—what makes them look like that?" I ask.

"The Withers virus attacks connective tissue. It's all throughout the body, in every system, which is why it's so deadly. But one of the more visible signs is when it dissolves the layer of cells holding the skin in place. Without that, the skin drops and stretches larger and larger as it's pulled by gravity. Even when people manage to survive the worst of the infection, their appearance is forever changed by it."

When we enter the Hospital Wing, more people descend on us with scanners and needles and vials of things I don't recognize. They're all dressed in clean, black-and-blue uniforms.

They try to lead the boy away, but he doesn't want to go, and I protest their efforts to take him. Finally, they give up trying to separate us, and let him stay curled up in a ball at the foot of my bed while they work on healing my leg, head, and myriad of other cuts and bruises.

"We need you to change into a medical gown so we

can treat your injuries," says Tella.

"Okay," I agree, and let her help me to my feet.

When the boy sees that I'm leaving, he moves to follow. I give him a hug and reassure him I'll be right back. Even though I don't think he understands my words, he settles back down and seems to accept that I'll return.

Tella leads me behind a curtain and helps me out of my scorched and soiled clothes. When she sees the infected gash on my leg, she gasps in shock. I glance down to get a peek at it, and it definitely looks worse than this morning. The center of the wound is charred and blackened from where it was cauterized to stop the bleeding, but the borders are less red and more purplish-black now, and dotted with goopy-looking blisters.

"This wound has been burned," Tella gasps, easily identifying that this burn is different from the fresh burns on my calves caused by the fire nipping at me as I fled. "What did this to you?"

"I did it to myself," I say. "Or rather, Vander did it, but only because I made him."

"Why would you do that?"

I roll my eyes, annoyed at her criticism of my survival medical skills. "I thought it was a better idea than bleeding to death."

That shuts her up.

She helps me back to the stretcher where the boy waits patiently and smiles upon my return.

Several other doctors gather around. They give me

something to make me sleep while they work on me, but it's not until I see Shawny and the others being rolled through the door that I'm finally able to fully surrender to unconsciousness—a blissful, painless escape.

*   *   *

I open my eyes to darkness and my pulse quickens, trying to remember where I am and what's happening. All at once, a recollection of the fire, the Roamers, and the hoverplane comes back to me. I sit up, expecting the familiar stab of pain in my leg that I've lived with for days now, but it doesn't come. My motion seems to trigger the lights, and the room illuminates with a gentle glow that's just the perfect brightness to allow me to see without straining my eyes.

I'm in a small room, just big enough for a bed and table. The boy isn't curled at the foot of my bed anymore, and I wonder where they've taken him. I can see the Hospital Wing through a window in the door. This must be a room for people who require extended care. I wonder how many days I'll need to be here recovering from my extensive injuries. It's odd that I can't feel any of them now. Whatever they gave me for pain must still be working.

I'm still wearing the flimsy white medical gown Tella helped me change into. I pull up the soft fabric to examine the place I was cut and find nothing but perfect flesh. I feel along the crown of my head for the spot where my skull slammed into a rock, but my touch elicits no pain. There's no bump or scab or any sign of trauma. I don't even have a headache. Whatever they did was far superior medical care than I ever could have gotten back home in the Smoke. I'm not sure even Doctor Hollen would have been capable of so completely healing such a nasty wound overnight without leaving a single trace.

Grinning, I leap to my feet and revel in the complete and utter lack of pain I experience. Then I go to change back into my clothes and find that clean clothes—simple gray pants and a blue shirt with buttons running down the front—have been left out for me on the table next to the bed. I find my old clothes wadded in a trash bin nearby. Hastily, I change into the new clean clothes. The only part of my old clothes I retain are the shoes—the ones Eason gave me. Before I slip them on my feet, I pull them to my chest and hold them as though they represent a piece of him. But soon I feel silly. I wipe away the tears streaking my cheeks and slip my feet into the soiled, blue shoes. Then I pull from my old pants' pockets the only two possessions of value I have left—the broken transmitter and the wadded mass of paper that was once Eason's note, before it was soaked in the rain.

The only sound I hear is the low, almost imperceptible hum of the hoverplane's engines. They're so much quieter inside than they are from the ground. Quietly, I tiptoe to the door and slide it open a crack to peek out. On the far side of the room, a window to the outside shows nothing but blackness. The earlier commotion has subsided, and now the central area of the Hospital Wing is deserted of everyone except Tella, who sits in a blue, metal chair, reading something on a tablet. I suppose the others have probably been moved to their own little rooms.

"Tella," I whisper.

She looks up, surprised. "Oh, it's you, Emery. How are you doing?"

I cross the room to her, and it's clear that my leg's improvement is more than skin-deep. If I hadn't seen the blisters and streaks of red or smelled the putrid odor of decay, I wouldn't believe there had ever been anything wrong with my leg.

"I'm doing great," I say. "My leg is all better."

She smiles. "Well, of course it is."

There's a slight swaying of the ground below me. "Are we still flying?"

"Yes, just a little farther."

"How long was I asleep?" I ask, wondering how far from The City they're taking us.

"It's nearly dawn. You slept for about eight hours."

I wonder how fast this hoverplane flies. How many hundreds of miles away from The City, and everyone I love, have I traveled? How can it be that when Whyle, Eason, and my parents need me the most, I'm farther away than any of us ever dreamed possible?

"When are we going back?" I demand.

"Soon," Tella assures me. "Right after we pick up the newest refugees from Twelve."

"Twelve?" I ask, not sure what she means by that.

"Safe Dome Twelve. We usually just call them by their numbers. It's too big a mouthful to say the whole thing every time. Anyway, I'm sure we'll be returning to Ten. That's where all the action is right now."

I don't know a lot about the other Safe Domes, but I do know there are twelve in total, and that The City was the tenth one built. I'm instantly brought back to a memory of Eason sitting across the dining hall table from me, telling me that they were all built by the Architect, who never entered one himself. Eason must have learned that from his father, who was on the Council before The City's artificial intelligence computer, Ember, secretly took over and expelled all but one member of the Council and cut off all communication with the outside world.

"What do you mean all of the action is in Ten?" I question.

She gnaws at her lower lip. "I want to show you something," she says, standing.

I follow her to the window and look out at the world.

"I love this view," she says. "This is my favorite part of the job. I could stand here for days."

I get the feeling she's trying to distract me from something she wasn't supposed to say—something about Ten. Even though I know this, it works. The sun is just cresting the horizon, casting the sky into brilliant blues and pinks and yellows. The sky is beautiful from the ground, but it's a whole other level of amazing when it's wrapped around you. It's so awe-inspiring that I nearly forget to breathe. We pass through clouds that seem to evaporate into white smoke the instant we touch them. From here, the ground and the trees don't even seem real. They look like miniature toys a child might play with, but even that makes them seem more tangible than they appear from so far above. I stare out as we soar over scattered trees and fields. But then the scene starts to shift below us.

"What's all that?" I ask, pointing at a large area where the ground appears littered with rubble.

"That used to be a city."

"How long ago?" If that was once a city, it must have been abandoned hundreds of years ago, considering how fully nature has swallowed and decayed anything that might have once been inhabitable buildings.

"It was abandoned during the height of the Withers epidemic." She rubs her chin, thinking. "I guess it's been about nineteen or twenty years."

I squint at the sight of the decayed city as it fades away into the distance. Is the outside world really so inhospitable that in two decades, a thriving city can be obliterated so completely through sheer neglect?

"There's Twelve," Tella says, pointing up ahead. "Do you see it?"

It takes my eyes a minute to separate the vibrant green trees from the unnatural green shimmer of the barrier field, as though it's camouflaged. There's no fire or ash surrounding this Safe Dome, just beautiful forests, meadows of flowers, and, on one side, a pool of water bigger than the entire dome.

"Is that the ocean?" I ask in amazement.

Tella chuckles. "Oh, no. That's just a lake. The ocean is thousands of times bigger than that."

My eyes widen. If that's true, then the Earth must be a lot bigger than I ever guessed just from reading about it in the illegal books I bartered from Kenna.

The plane begins to hover near Twelve, just as it did when they picked us up last night. Even though I'm expecting it, and I know they'll be fine, my stomach flutters anxiously as three masked men jump from the hoverplane and float down to the ground. It's only then that I remember the golden bracelets that were placed on me. I check my wrists and ankles, but they've been removed. Honestly, I hope I never have to wear them again.

"What exactly are we doing here?" I ask.

"We got word that there are more refugees coming out of Twelve."

"Refugees?"

"People who have been expelled from the Safe Dome—like you and your companions."

"Does that happen often?"

"That's the strange thing," Tella says, her voice taking on a quiet, conspiratorial tone. "Eventually, every Safe Dome has begun expelling people, just as yours did to the five of you last night—though not always in such a rough, dramatic way. In fact, you five are the first to be expelled from your dome, so yours was the last to undertake the practice. Ten is also the only one that we've seen develop a double-layered city—a Safe Dome within a Safe Dome, so to speak. It's really fascinating. But every Safe Dome has its peculiarities."

"And you all pick up the people who are expelled?"

"Yes. And we're working to deactivate the Safe Domes for good and free everyone."

I want to ask more about that, but before I have a chance—

"What's going on?" asks a groggy voice. We turn to see Ty standing barefoot in the open doorway to his room, his red hair disheveled from sleep.

"Ty, how are you?" I ask, rushing over to him.

He grins widely. "I'm fantastic. How about you?"

"Great. Whatever they did to my leg completely healed it."

"Blazes, that's great," he replies.

"How about you?" I ask tentatively. "Were they able to… What do you think…" I want to know if he's still under the effects of the Mind Mist, and I'm not sure how to ask. *Were they able to fix your brain?* Honestly, if they weren't, Ty would be the last person to realize it. "Did they say anything is wrong?" I finally manage.

"One of the doctors said there's something… How did he put it? Oh yeah, fuzzing my brain." He rolls his eyes as he says this, as though he doesn't believe a word of it. "He said it should wear off in a few days, and we'll just have to wait it out. I'm not sure what he's talking about, because I feel great."

I sigh in relief. Ty may not be back to himself yet, but

the doctors think he will be soon. I can live with that. "Well, hang in there."

He gives me a double thumbs-up. "No problem there. Like I said, I feel fantastic."

Suddenly, the Hospital Wing erupts into a hailstorm of activity.

CHAPTER 3

Three people in the black-and-blue uniforms of the SDRT enter, escorting a boy and a girl who appear about my age. They wear clothing that looks as though it came straight out of Keya's closet back in the Flame—smooth, colorful, and sparkling fabrics. But their clothes and their faces are dirty and rumpled, so they must be the refugees we're here to pick up. The girl carries a bag at her waist, but otherwise they don't appear to have brought anything with them.

Several of the medical staff try to separate them, just like they did with me and the boy last night, but the girl cries and fights so vehemently that the doctors finally agree to let them stay together.

The next problem comes when Doctor Gill tries to examine them. Tentatively, they let her look them over for injuries and feel for pulses at their necks, but when she approaches them with a scanner, things change. The boy leaps protectively in front of the girl and says, "That won't be necessary. We're both perfectly fine."

"This won't harm you," Doctor Gill stammers, taken aback by his refusal.

"I said that's enough. We're fine," the boy repeats.

"All right," Doctor Gill replies, and sets the scanner down slowly, clearly dealing with someone who isn't entirely rational. "What are your names?"

"My name is Aiken, and this is…"

"I'm Mara," the girl says, cutting him off.

"You're not Mara," the boy mutters, exasperated.

At this, the girl—who may or may not be Mara—bursts into sobs, and the boy sighs and puts a consoling arm around her, patting her shoulder. This seems to calm her, and she nestles against his chest.

This is drama I don't need to be involved in. Back in the Smoke, I used to be good at staying out of other people's business because it only tends to make their problems bleed all over you. Lately I haven't been so good at that, and I need to get back to it. So instead of listening any further, I look for my people.

Vander and Kamella stand off by themselves in the far corner of the Hospital Wing. I'm sure they've both been healed just as well as I have. Kamella's skin looks flawless, but apparently there's nothing they could do for her hair; it hangs in uneven, short, black, frizzy clumps. Somehow she still looks beautiful, even though she's tugging at her hair and crying. Vander has an arm around her and is trying to comfort her.

I decide to leave the two of them alone for now and check on Shawny. I peek through the windows into the private rooms until I find her. She's sitting up, so I tap gently at the door and slide it open.

"Hi, Shawny! How are you?" I ask tentatively.

She looks up and smiles. "I'm great! Would you like to meet Quinn?" She uncovers the little bundle in her arms and beckons me over.

I don't have a lot of experience with newborn babies. I was nine when Whyle was born, and I'm trying to remember if his face looked quite so purple and wrinkled that first time I saw him. But then this little guy makes the faintest sigh, and the sound is so precious that I'm instantly in love with him—bald head, squished face and all.

"Quinn," I coo, reaching out to stroke his soft little head. "What were the names of your other kids?" I ask her. "Weren't they similar?"

"I have Finn, who's six, and Wren, who's four. When we get back in The City, this little guy will fit right in with his big brother and sister," she says, stroking the backs of her fingertips across his little cheek.

I pull up a chair to sit next to her. "Shawny, did they say anything to you about plans to get back in The City?" I whisper. Maybe someone told her more than I managed to get out of Tella.

"Isn't that what this group's whole mission is?"

"But how long have they been trying?" I ask. "I get the feeling that all the Safe Domes are still active, so they don't seem to really know what they're doing."

Shawny sighs and looks down at her little baby. "I guess we'll just have to wait and see. But at least we're safe today." I nod, comforted by her calm assurance, almost as if my own mother were here. "Though your blazingly ludicrous plan nearly got us all killed, we're still here," she adds.

I groan and stand to leave, all traces of comfort erased by her overly honest way of putting things.

I exit her room just in time to see General Rockshire enter the Hospital Wing. He looks different without the cumbersome mask he wore on the ground, but I recognize his eyes, hazel and warm. He's leading in another refugee—a man who looks to be in his early twenties with a thin face and wiry build. The man keeps fighting against his rescuer's hold, but it looks like it's more for show than an actual attempt at escape.

"We found one more lurking in the woods."

"Oh, my!" exclaims Doctor Gill. "Thank you, General Rockshire." To the agitated man, she says, "We're here to help you. No need to be afraid."

"If you take me, who's going to keep an eye on Sanctuary?" he cries.

"The best thing you can do for your Safe Dome is to come with us and share what you know," Doctor Gill assures him. "What's your name?"

The man ignores her and runs over to the boy and girl whose names I've already forgotten. "Mara, Aiken, tell them. Something's wrong with Sanctuary. And where did all the others disappear to?"

"Toren, calm down," Aiken says, slipping out of Maybe-Mara's grip.

"If you're talking about the other twenty people who were recently exiled from Twelve, we picked them up a few days ago," says General Rockshire. "They'd traveled several miles away to find food. It seems it was only the three of you who remained near your city."

With all the commotion, the young boy—I wish I had a name for him—has finally woken and stands in the doorway of his room. His expression is frightened until his eyes finally land on me. With a smile, he scurries over and nestles himself against my side. I'm not sure exactly what I did to earn this boy's trust and become his protector, but I wrap an arm around him and whisper reassurances anyway.

The ground beneath us shifts, eliciting a yelp from me and several of the other new arrivals. The hoverplane is breaking from its stationary hover over Twelve and accelerating away.

"Stop! We can't leave," Aiken exclaims. "You promised you could get into Sanctuary." He runs to the door, and I wonder if he plans to try and get off the hoverplane.

General Rockshire puts out an arm to stop him, and Aiken is no match for the general's imposing force. "We will, but it's going to take time."

"I'm not leaving Mara," Aiken insists.

The girl bursts into sobs all over again, her long blond hair sweeping across her face as she slumps under this strange sorrow. "Aiken, *I'm* Mara," she whispers, her voice pleading.

He ignores her words, takes her hand, and leads her from the room.

"How much time?" I demand.

General Rockshire turns and looks at me with an impassive gaze. "As long as it takes."

Earlier, Tella made it sound like they might have a way to get back into The City soon—before it's too late for Whyle and Eason. But General Rockshire's words imply no immediate action or urgency.

A feeling of panic starts to well up. "We have to deactivate the barrier field. The City's computer is an artificial intelligence named Ember that has completely taken over, and no one is safe," I say, begging him to understand and do something.

He smiles sympathetically, but doesn't look alarmed. "Oh, we know all about the computers. We've known for a long time. What do you think we've been doing all these years? Each of the domes has its own version—each a little different, but all tyrannical."

"So what's your plan? Tella mentioned..." In my periphery I see Tella's eyes widen, and she gives an infinitesimal shake of her head. I let my words trail off, not wanting to get her in trouble for saying something she wasn't supposed to. "Well, anyway...what's your plan?"

Vander and Kamella have drifted over to join the conversation.

"We may be able to help," Vander says. "We've learned some important things about The City recently."

Doctor Gill walks up behind him. "That's good," she says with an approving nod. "I know Commander Elben is anxious to speak with all of you. But first, it's time for breakfast. Please follow me." With that, she turns and strides to the door.

"Excuse me, Doctor Gill," one of the staff members calls. "Can I have a word? It's about"—he eyes us uncertainly—"the research," he finally finishes.

"Oh, certainly," she says. "General, I suppose you can handle this on your own."

"I'll try to manage, and I'll call you if things get out of hand," he replies dryly, and it's difficult to tell if he's joking or not.

Ty, Vander, Kamella, Shawny, Toren, the young boy, and I all follow the general down the hallway. We look like the procession marching through the streets of the Flame to enter the Burning. But this is just breakfast, not a contest for our right to remain.

We enter another brightly lit room, crowded with tables and people—most of them around my parents' age, by the look of it, and almost all dressed in SDRT uniforms. A long line snakes along the wall and between tables where people sit eating. I try not to bump anyone's head as we join the queue.

Kamella runs her hand nervously through her unsightly hair, glancing around. I notice the furtive glances some people give her and can't help feeling sorry for her. I remember when it was Eason and me who were the recipients of loaded glances in the Burning Center.

Rather than wait with us, General Rockshire disappears out the door.

The crowded room and loud noises exacerbate the boy's fears, and he clings tighter to my side. I wish I knew what to do for him, but I can't say I've ever been great with kids. Well, except Whyle, but he was better with me than I was with him.

"Can you do this?" Kamella asks the child in her sweet, sing-song voice that's naturally calm and comforting. She does a little clapping rhythm with her hands, smiling warmly, forgetting her own insecurities.

I roll my eyes; no one wants to play a silly clapping game she probably invented under the influence of the Mind Mist. But to my surprise, the boy breaks free of me for just long enough to repeat the rhythm. Then he hides his face behind me again.

"That was perfect," Kamella praises.

He peeks out to give her a smile before hiding again. We take a few steps forward as the line moves closer to the serving table.

"Can you do this one?" She claps a new rhythm, just slightly longer and more complicated.

The boy steps out and tries to repeat the rhythm, but makes a few mistakes near the end. He sets his features in a look of determination and gestures for her to repeat the pattern. His next attempt is flawless.

When we step forward in line, he slides closer to Kamella, ready for another pattern. The next one she shows him requires both of them to slap their hands together. It doesn't take long for him to understand, and soon they're clapping and slapping hands together in perfect tempo. Kamella is singing a little chant to the rhythm, and the boy is laughing.

Vander and I exchange a surprised glance.

"I told you we needed her," Vander whispers.

"Maybe," I say noncommittally.

Even though I was fully against his decision to give the last dose of the Mind Mist antidote to Kamella instead of Ty—who has information about the Resistance inside The City—I have to admit she's been surprisingly helpful from the start. And it turns out her ridiculously sweet demeanor wasn't just a product of the mist, but is just how she really is. I'm not ready to admit any of this out loud to Vander, but I can tell by the smug look on his face that he already knows.

When we reach the front of the line, a woman wearing a net over her gray curly hair says in a staccato monotone, "Welcome aboard. We have two choices for breakfast: eggs with toast or toast with eggs. What will it be?"

I stare at her blankly, not sure what to make of that.

"Eggs with toast sounds lovely," Kamella says enthusiastically.

"Wait," Toren says. "What kind of eggs are those?"

"Chicken eggs," the woman replies.

Eyes squinted, Toren leans forward to inspect the eggs on a plate, sniffing them suspiciously. "And where exactly do you keep the chickens on board?"

The woman shoves seven identical trays toward us, each containing two slices of thick toast and a big scoop of scrambled eggs. It's only from my time in the Flame and on the farm that I'm able to identify these things.

We each take a tray and look for a place to sit. To say

that the tables are full would be an understatement. Long benches line the five tables running the length of the room, and everyone just squeezes in.

Rather than shove my way in at a table next to the others, where everyone has to turn their trays sideways just to make them fit, I slip out into the hallway and sit on the floor outside the door.

In the open space, I inhale deeply and start shoveling the food into my mouth. It's a little on the bland side compared to the food on the farm, but nothing can be worse than the gray mush I was raised on back in the Smoke. Now that the farm is part of The City, will people be able to get better food, or will Ember find a way to stop them and force them to consume the meal rations that are selectively poisoning people with a certain gene— a gene my brother carries?

Whatever the SDRT has discovered about the Safe Domes better work quickly, because people like Whyle may not have much time left. All my efforts to cross the Wall of Fire and get Curosene for him only prolonged his life by a few weeks. Any day now Whyle could fall ill again, and this time there won't be more Curosene to bring him back.

"Cafeteria a bit crowded this morning?" someone asks.

I look up to see a man who's probably in his mid-thirties, with dark skin and a gentle smile. "You could say that," I mutter.

I expect him to pass by and go inside for his own breakfast, but instead, he crouches down next to me.

"New here?"

I nod.

"So does that make you from Ten or Twelve?" he asks, his speech affected in a drawn-out way I've never heard before.

"Ten. How about you?"

"Two," he replies.

"How long ago did they pick you up?" I ask around a mouthful of eggs.

"Almost a week. They keep saying they're going to take me to a new city of survivors, but then they keep dragging me all over the place picking up new people."

"Are there a lot of survivors?" I ask.

"Not a lot. We've run into a few, but as far as I can tell most of the old cities are abandoned and crumbling. Most of the survivors are from down south where the weather is warmer. The disease didn't thrive as well there as it did in the cooler climates further north."

The sound of footsteps clicking down the hallway draws my gaze, and I turn to see General Rockshire leading Aiken and Mara to the cafeteria. They don't seem to find the prospect of breakfast nearly as objectionable as the medical exam. The general nods once in our direction and proceeds inside without a word, so I take that to mean I'm free to eat my meals in the hallway if I choose.

"Excuse my ill manners," the man says. "I never asked your name."

"Emery Kennish. And yours?"

"Keaton Branson," he replies, holding out a hand to

shake mine.

"Nice to meet you."

"Likewise."

"So what was it like in your Safe Dome?" I ask. "I get the feeling they're all different somehow."

"Seems like it. My city is called Reprieve and it's... Well, it's a little hard to describe. Let's just say society's not as orderly or safe as it is here."

"So what does that mean? Are there a lot of criminals?"

"Not exactly. To have criminals you need laws, which we don't really have. The core value of Reprieve is that the highest moral is the desire of the individual."

"So people can just do whatever they want?" I ask in astonishment, scarcely able to imagine what a society without rules would be like and whether or not it would be a good thing.

"Basically," says Keaton.

"And that works?"

He shrugs. "Depends on what you mean by 'works.' Two people rarely have the same idea about how things should be, and when those conflict, there's no legitimate way to solve the problem. So, it's really just a matter of the strong against the weak."

Compared to that, The City doesn't seem so bad suddenly. Well, except the part about Ember trying to kill my brother and holding Eason hostage. But besides that, at least you can count on food and work, and you can walk through the streets in relative safety.

It wasn't that long ago that these things were all I

wanted out of life. I could have been perfectly content to stay in the Smoke and live out my dreary days one by one until my face grew as worn as my mother's. But it's amazing how quickly things can change. It still sends my head spinning to think how my split-second decision to illegally cross the Wall of Fire irrevocably changed the course of my life forever—no going back.

"Doesn't sound like a very nice place, but you seem nice enough," I say.

"Well, I'm old enough to remember a time before the Safe Domes. My mother died of the Withers while trying to get me to safety. She'd have rolled over in her grave if I threw away everything she taught me just because I ended up in a crazed shelter."

"You said you could *almost* do whatever you want. So what couldn't you do?" I ask.

"Organize."

"What?" I say, confused.

"That's what got me kicked out. Turns out, I was lucky in that regard—out's way better than in, these days. But we aren't allowed to form groups and cooperate. I wasn't trying to cause trouble. I just realized that we could live better and more peacefully if we quit fighting and tried to work together. When I started talking about it, a lot of people wanted to join me—realizing that even the weak could be strong together. And before I knew it, Central Computing had deactivated my ID. My choice at that point was either to starve to death or leave. I chose to take my chances out here."

"Is Central Computing the computer that runs your city?"

"Yeah, like your… What did they say its name was?"

"Ember," I say, amazed at how fast word travels on a ship like this.

"Wait, wasn't your name…"

"Emery," I say. "Totally different."

He gives me a long look, as though the fact that my name happens to be similar to that monster's makes me somehow connected to it.

I scowl, but let it go, more interested in what I'm learning about the other Safe Domes. I have plenty of questions, but before I have a chance to ask anything else, General Rockshire exits the cafeteria leading all the refugees from Ten and Twelve, along with the child.

"Time for your meeting with Commander Elben," he says.

If I'm looking for answers, this is where I'm going to get them. Suddenly feeling anxious, I get to my feet. "Keaton, it was nice talking to you. I guess I'll see you around."

He nods and stands as well.

The general takes my tray and hands it Ty, who passes it along down the line until it's been returned back to the cafeteria for me.

"Thanks," I mutter, a little startled.

"You'd better come along too, Keaton," says General Rockshire.

"Oh, no. You didn't get any breakfast," I say, feeling

bad for taking up all his time.

"That's okay. They served toast and eggs, and I only like eggs and toast," he says with a wink.

"Follow me," the general instructs, and marches off toward what I hope will be answers and good news for everyone back in The City.

CHAPTER 4

We're brought to a simple room with a large oval table surrounded by a dozen chairs. There's nothing frilly or decorative; this space is all business.

"Wait here," says General Rockshire when we're all inside, and he departs.

I take a seat next to Shawny, with Quinn a little bundle in her arms. The boy is on my other side, between Kamella and me. It doesn't take long before he starts to fidget.

"Gar, it's okay," Kamella says in a soothing tone, patting his arm.

"What did you call him?" I ask.

"Gar. It's his name. At least, I think it is," says Kamella. "When I told him my name, he pointed to himself and said 'Gar.' And he seems to like it when I call him that."

"Gar," I say to the boy.

He smiles and nods. I marvel at Kamella's skill with this child—and honestly, with people in general.

"Emery," I say, pointing to myself.

"Eerry," he mumbles, trying to imitate my word.

Mara and Aiken sit across from us, observing without saying a word. Mara loops her arm through his and nestles her head on his shoulder, which he appears to merely tolerate, returning none of her affection.

We wait in silence for several minutes.

"So are they just going to keep us here forever?" Vander complains, breaking the strained silence.

"I think General Rockshire went to get Commander Elben," Keaton says.

"Well, they're certainly taking their time about it," Vander mutters.

I can't blame him for being annoyed and anxious. I feel it, too. Every moment that passes without knowing what's happening back in The City is like being gnawed on by a million rats—every one of them a different kind of worry. What else has Ember done to The City—to our families—now that she's revealed her existence? I think of her pale skin and cold, dark eyes—beautiful and chilling—and I shudder. To restore order, I expect she would do almost anything. I have imagined far too many awful things. It must be easy for her to see people as nothing more than cogs in her machine, since she doesn't have a soul.

Fortunately, that's when the door opens, and I'm able to rip my imagination back from the precipice it threatens to tumble over. General Rockshire enters, followed by Commander Elben, who walks like he owns the world.

At his appearance, Mara stiffens and opens her mouth to speak. But Aiken grabs her arm and gives a minuscule shake of his head, warning her to stay silent, which she does.

Without any introduction or explanation, Commander Elben takes a seat at the head of the table and launches into a tirade of questions, wanting to know everything we can tell him about the inner workings of our Safe Domes and the exact events that led to our expulsion. He focuses his questions on me and my companions—seeming to already be aware of what's happening in the other domes. That must be because Keaton has been here for a while and I heard the general say they recently picked up other refugees from Twelve, where Aiken, Mara, and Toren come from. I try to get through our story as quickly as possible so we can get to the part where they finally give us answers about how we're going to get back in The City.

When I get to the part about Eason's attempts to trigger the Safe Dome's deactivation protocol—the plan that sent me to the Ash—I pull the broken transmitter from my pocket and show it to them.

"That explains the signal we picked up," says General Rockshire, inspecting the punctured silver sphere. "It had been a while since we made runs over Ten, but when that signal went out, we decided it was time to check in again."

"Can you fix it? Can you read the signal and use it to deactivate The City's barrier field?" I ask, hopeful.

Commander Elben takes the small device and inspects it for a moment. "It's not likely this can be repaired. And once it lost power, it would have lost its transmission settings. It won't be any further use to us." He sets the transmitter on the table. "Besides, we haven't picked up any signals coming out of Ten in over twenty-four hours. It seems that the matching signal has been turned off."

I cover my mouth and stifle a gasp. Does that mean Ember finally made Eason tell her his plan? If the transmitter in The City has been found and deactivated, will she have any need to keep Eason? And if not, will she simply expel him the way she did the five of us, or will she kill him the way she's doing to Whyle and others like him?

"It's no matter, though," Commander Elben goes on, unconcerned. "It seems that activating it within the dome had some effect on the barrier field. This may have turned the tides of the whole rescue operation in our favor."

"Really," Vander and I say in unison, desperate to believe all our efforts and sacrifices actually accomplished something in the end.

"How so?" says Keaton.

Commander Elben waves his hand dismissively. "A lot of boring details we don't need to get into, but our researchers are working on it. We'll know more in a few days." He stands. "I suppose that's all the use you can be to me. We're transporting you all to Blue Haven as we speak, and we'll be arriving shortly."

"About time," Keaton mutters.

"Wait, where's that?" Vander asks.

"It's not much farther, a thriving city where we've

been gathering survivors and refugees for the last few years. It's the pinnacle of human achievement—a true utopia. You'll be safe there," Commander Elben explains with pride, as though he's personally responsible for it.

"Pardon me," says Toren, "but we've all been promised that before, and it didn't exactly turn out to be true. There's no way you're putting me in another Safe Dome."

Murmurs of agreement ripple around the room.

"This isn't a Safe Dome," General Rockshire interjects. "It's completely open, and you're free to come and go as you please. You'll be taken care of there."

"What about the Roamers and the Withers?" Shawny asks, holding Quinn just a little closer.

"Roamers know to steer clear of all the new cities like Blue Haven. We guard the perimeter well," Commander Elben assures her. "There has never been a case of the Withers inside Blue Haven, and we intend on keeping it that way."

"I'm not going to this new Black Handle place, or whatever it's called," I say.

"Blue Haven," the general repeats dryly.

I ignore him. "I want to go back to The City."

"Blue Haven is a city," General Rockshire replies patiently.

"Not *a* city. *The* City. My city. Safe Dome Ten." This is the first time it occurs to me how silly, and maybe a little arrogant, it was for us to call our city "The City," as though it was the only city left in existence. But for the past twenty-two years, it has been the only city that existed in our accessible world, so perhaps it makes sense. "I want to stay here and do whatever I can until that computer and the Safe Dome are destroyed, once and for all."

Commander Elben laughs. "That's out of the question. I can assure you the best thing you can do is go to Blue Haven and stay out of the way while we rescue your families."

"And how long has this rescue mission been underway?" Vander asks.

"We began the process seven years ago," Commander Elben replies.

"And how many Safe Domes still stand?" Toren asks skeptically.

"We're getting very close to completing the mission," the commander replies, annoyed and purposely vague.

"How many?" I repeat, forcing him to admit the situation aloud.

"At this point, eleven Safe Domes are still operational," General Rockshire informs us.

Honestly, that's a lower number than any of us were expecting, and we gasp in surprise and hope. If they've deactivated one, maybe there really is a chance for the rest.

"Which one is free?" Shawny asks.

"Safe Dome One," says Commander Elben. "And we're very close to finding a way into the others."

"I say blast them to bits," Toren chimes in.

"We've tried bombings, but the Safe Domes are too strong for that," General Rockshire replies. "We've also considered EMPs."

"What are those?" asks Kamella.

"Electromagnetic pulse. An energy blast strong enough to disable any electronic device in range. The problem is that every Safe Dome has constructed some form of protective shield against such an attack. In Ten, for example, that Wall of Fire dividing the city is made of an energy that repels such a pulse and protects the computer system. In Twelve, it's a metal shielding in the tall tower at the center of the city. We're told that's where their governor lives, and where all important city business takes place."

Mara and Aiken nod, but still add nothing to the conversation.

I feel my earlier hopes starting to plummet. These people may have good intentions, but they've been fighting this battle for seven years with very little to show for it. They need someone who understands how the A.I. really works.

"We need to find the Architect," I say, drawing the gaze of everyone in the room. "The person who built the Safe Domes. He'll know how to deactivate the computers and the barrier fields. I was told he never entered a Safe Dome himself." When Eason told me this, it seemed sad that the creator of the Safe Domes never managed to reach the safety they offered, but now I wonder if maybe he knew something was wrong with his creations from the very beginning. Still, whoever he is, he must know how to shut them down.

"We've already found the Architect," Commander Elben says in a slow, measured tone.

My pulse quickens. "Really? Where is he? I want to talk to him."

He smiles a slow, twisted smile that's anything but friendly. "Fine, I'll go get him for you." He exits the room, leaving a humming charge in the silence as we wait.

Everyone appears slightly on edge except the general, whose face is completely unreadable. I'm sure everyone in this room has some questions—and maybe a few curses—for the person who created the prisons that promised to keep us safe.

A few moments later, Commander Elben returns alone.

"Where is he?" I demand, wondering if the Architect is refusing to face us.

He smiles patronizingly and holds up his arms. "Surprise, it's me."

"You?" we all mutter in unison.

I grit my teeth, infuriated that no one saw fit to share this detail with us. I turn to General Rockshire. "And are you secretly the creator of the Withers?" He stares back, unamused. I press on. "Do you have any parents, children, uncles, or second cousins we should be aware of?" I say, and stare him down so he knows I mean business.

Everyone's staring at me as if I'm not entirely sane.

And perhaps I *am* going crazy. My mind is hazy, and I don't feel fully connected to the rest of my body. Maybe after everything I've endured, I really am going mad.

I see Vander snickering in my periphery, but I don't break eye contact with the general.

Finally, he gives in. "My grandfather was the secretary to the last president, but he's been dead for years. And I have an aunt who's somewhat well known for telling stories in Blue Haven. But there's no one else of fame or notoriety in my family who I'm aware of."

I nod approvingly. I'm done finding out far too late that people aren't who I thought. Like when I learned Beatie was actually Bretton Crandell, councilman. And Ollie and Roe were also members of the former Council. Or that people have family connections that cast all of their actions and motives in an entirely new light, like when I discovered Eason and Kamella were the children of Council members. Or when Doctor Hollen pretended he would report the assault I sustained in the maze trial at the hands of Vander, who turned out to be his son and identical twins.

"So you created the Safe Domes and the computer system that runs them?" Keaton asks, sounding much more rational and less accusatory than me. I can see how he would have the right demeanor to unite people.

"Yes," says Commander Elben, all traces of humor gone. "I am the Architect. But if I weren't, you can bet I would have already found him. If anyone can bring down those Safe Domes, it's me. So you can put any notions of coming in here and saving the day out of your heads. There's nothing you know that I don't know, nothing you can say that I haven't already thought of, and nothing you can do to help except to *get out of the way*." He puts special emphasis on each of the last words.

"So if you made these…whatever they are that have taken over the cities, why don't you just shut them off?" Kamella asks, the frustration in her tone sounding out of place in her lilting cadence.

"The fact that you would ask that question shows how little you understand the technology at work here," says Commander Elben. "These are complex artificial intelligences. Nothing like them has ever existed in the history of the world. I will shut them down. It just has to be done delicately so we don't destroy anything important," Commander Elben explains as though he's talking to a child—a very young, very stupid child.

His arrogance is insufferable.

"You can't just dump us somewhere," I protest. "We know the Safe Domes. We've been inside; you haven't. You need us."

He gives one sharp shake of his head. "That's completely out of the question. I can handle this just fine without you. You're going to Blue Haven this afternoon, and that's final."

The room erupts in dissent, but Commander Elben turns back to General Rockshire, already dismissing us completely.

I'm not ready to give up, though. I leap to my feet, my

voice rising with me. "You listen here!" I exclaim, ready to truly let him know what I think of him and his ability to take care of a problem—considering he's the one who created it.

Shawny, who sits between me and Commander Elben cradling her baby, stands and places one hand on my shoulder. "Emery," she says in a calming tone, "getting so upset isn't going to solve this. Take a deep breath."

I'm not happy about it, but I do as she instructs. The rest of the room quiets as well.

"Good," she says. "Now hold the baby." She passes the tiny person wrapped in soft blankets to me, and I wonder if she thinks that holding him will soothe me. But as soon as her hands are free of him, she rounds on Commander Elben, pulls him by the shoulder so he turns back to face her, and puts a stern finger inches from his nose. "Now you listen here," she says, all pretense of calm instantly vanished. "I don't know what made you think you had the right to play god with other people's lives, but that all ended the moment you lost control of that fire-shooting, demon computer. You might have created The City, but we're the ones who lived there. It's our families still trapped there. We *are* going back, and if you have a problem with it, you're welcome to go bide your time waiting around in Blue Haven, but we're all staying right here until this is finished." With that, Shawny sits and holds out her arms for Quinn.

Smiling, I relinquish him to her care. A sense of finality permeates the air, as though her words have decided the matter for everyone. I can hardly believe I ever questioned whether giving Shawny the antidote was the right decision.

Commander Elben opens his mouth to say something, and from the look on his face, he isn't about to acquiesce, but Shawny cuts him off. "General Rockshire, I believe we have plans to discuss—something about new research on crossing the barrier field."

I see the faintest hint of a smile in the general's eyes as he nods, the change in the atmosphere palpable.

Finally, Commander Elben huffs in irritation, his power-hold on this operation diminished by a fiery woman who's even shorter than he is. "Suit yourselves," he growls. "I have more important things to do than stay here arguing with children." And he turns and stalks out the door.

General Rockshire pushes up the sleeve of his right arm, revealing an odd silver rectangle. It looks like it's just a coloring of his skin, but when he touches it, lights and letters appear on its surface. He taps it a few times and says, "Doctor Gill."

"Yes?" her voice comes back through the device implanted on his arm.

"Can you come to the conference room? It's time to tell our guests what you've discovered."

CHAPTER 5

The only sounds while we wait for Doctor Gill are the claps of a new version of the hand game Kamella plays to entertain Gar. Soon Ty joins in, as well. The rest of us wait in tense silence.

Finally Doctor Gill enters, slightly winded and cradling a small black box to her chest. I remember seeing it earlier in the Hospital Wing, but hadn't paid it much attention at the time.

"So let's hear it. What's the big discovery?" Vander asks.

Even though Vander has Kamella here with him, I know he's every bit as dedicated to bringing down the Safe Dome as I am. I haven't doubted this since the moment he told me his identical twin brother is still trapped in The City. For their entire lives, they convinced everyone that the two of them were actually one single person because one more child was all their parents were allowed to have. But when they failed the Burning, Vander was sent to the Ash, and his twin, Van, was left behind—his intercuff deactivated, with no access to food and no right to exist at all.

Doctor Gill sets the box on the table and takes a deep

breath, smiling widely. "I can't tell you how excited I am about this breakthrough," she says, rocking from her heels to her toes and back again.

"How about you just tell us what it is and we'll decide how to feel about it," Toren mutters.

His impatience does nothing to curb her enthusiasm. "You see, every barrier field has some degree of permeability. Of course, we've known this. Typically it's been limited to certain gases, such as oxygen. But it was the rain last week that was our first clue something had changed in Ten. It went right through the barrier field. It hadn't done that before."

"Really?" I ask in surprise. The rainstorm that came one night after we activated the transmitter was the first I'd experienced in the Ash, so I'd assumed it was always like that. "Is that what changed when we activated the transmitter?"

"What transmitter?" Doctor Gill asks, not having been present for that part of the conversation.

I fill her in, noticing that, at some point, Mara has picked up the broken transmitter and is inspecting it carefully. I make a mental note to get it back later. It might not have any use, but it's still a piece of Eason that I don't want to lose.

"Fascinating," whispers Doctor Gill. "That must have been the catalyst for enhanced permeability. Before that, only atmospheric water vapor could permeate the barrier. Additional water was drawn from underground. But beginning a few days ago, we noticed that whole raindrops could get through. We began testing what else could suddenly enter the Safe Dome and found other substances could pass through the barrier, even some plants and animals."

"Have any of the other domes been similarly affected?" Aiken asks, of course thinking of his own home in Twelve.

"Not that we've been able to detect," says Doctor Gill regretfully. "This appears to be an isolated occurrence, which makes sense, given what Emery just told us about this transmitter." Aiken grimaces and nods soberly. Doctor Gill goes on. "So far, we've discovered that bananas, cotton seeds, a certain species of dung beetle, and rats are able to cross the barrier."

At the mention of rats, Vander and I exchange a glance and shudder, remembering the recent days when a few roasted rats were all that stood between us and starvation.

"Our planes are making drops on Ten to test out additional substances," explains Doctor Gill.

That explains all the hoverplanes that have been flying over The City. The first time Vander and I saw them, they dropped explosives. But over the next couple of days, they flew over several times and dropped other things. Some made it through, but most just bounced or rolled off.

"While I expect we'll continue to find more, it may not be necessary. I've recently had a breakthrough that may make it possible to get people through the barrier field, just given what we already know."

That's when Quinn starts to cry.

"I'll go take care of him," Shawny says, getting to her feet. And to me she whispers, "I want to hear everything I miss, and don't let them get away with any shenanigans."

"I promise," I whisper back with a smile.

When she's gone, along with the screeching cry of the bundle she cradles, Doctor Gill jumps right back into her explanation. "I've developed this compound." She opens the black box in front of her and holds up a single syringe filled with a pale yellow liquid. "It's called DS10, which stands for DNA Shift Ten because of what it does and the Safe Dome it targets. When this is injected into a person, it causes the cells to take on properties of another organism. The shift appears to be enough to allow for passage through the barrier field."

"You've tested this successfully?" Toren asks.

"So far we've gotten seven different species of vegetables, a cat, a bird, and two monkeys inside Ten using DS10," she replies. "The monkeys were wearing dive bands, which we were able to use to bring them back afterward."

"What are dive bands?" asks Vander.

"The wrist and ankle bands that brought you up to the aircraft," says General Rockshire. "They're reversible. Silver side out allows you to descend safely to the ground. Gold side out brings you up as far as there's somewhere for you to land. No one thought Doctor Gill would be able to teach monkeys to reverse them, but she did it."

I try to imagine what people in The City must be

thinking as vegetables, cats, and monkeys rain down on them. I wonder how many people have tried in vain to escape, thinking this signaled that the barrier field was no more. But perhaps not many, considering The City is still surrounded by a ring of blazing fire.

"How can you shift DNA without killing the organism?" Mara asks, her expression and tone far more rational and focused than I've seen her thus far.

"That's the amazing thing about what I've managed to do here," says Doctor Gill with pride. "It's a little tricky to explain."

Mara leans forward. "Try me," she says with complete confidence. There's clearly a side to Mara I don't understand. Though, honestly, it's not as though I understand anything about this girl or the boy she seems to love who keeps insisting that she isn't Mara at all.

"This compound inserts pieces of the target DNA into the cells of the host subject. They exist within the cells, which is enough to trick the barrier field, but they aren't actually incorporated into the host's DNA until…"

"Until the cells reproduce," says Mara, clearly understanding all of this much better than I am.

"Exactly," says Doctor Gill with an approving nod.

"But the resulting DNA would be unsustainable," says Mara. "The new DNA would be inserted randomly. Depending on what the insertions are, they would be cancerous at best and lethal at worst."

Doctor Gill doesn't deny it. "In one monkey, we were able to reverse the effects with a dose of Curosene." She pulls a small, familiar vial from the box.

My ears perk up at the mention of Curosene, amazed at what a vital role that drug has played in my life of late.

"What happened to the other monkey?" Toren asks.

Doctor Gill looks down. "That one we didn't give Curosene to, and it died after twelve hours."

Undeterred, I say, "So when do we send people in?"

"I estimate we'll be ready in three, maybe four weeks," says Doctor Gill with pride, as though this is good news.

"Weeks?" I exclaim. "What are you waiting for? Don't you realize how much danger everyone is in?"

General Rockshire steps forward. "Emery, we're very well aware of how serious this situation is, and that's why we have to be careful. There's no point sending people in until we have a plan in place to actually shut down the computer system. Without that, all we're doing is sacrificing our own people."

"Then I'll volunteer," says Vander, echoing my own thoughts. "If you're not willing to take the risk, then send me."

"Or me," I say.

"Or I'll do it," Kamella says, surprising me. I've been so focused on my own fears and reasons for needing to get back in The City, I never stopped to consider that Kamella has people she must be worried about, too—friends from the farm, and parents who were instrumental in organizing the rebellion in the Ash. They must be prime targets now.

General Rockshire raises a single eyebrow in a rare

showing of surprise, as though he didn't expect our dedication to this cause to run so deep. After all, how many people would volunteer to have their DNA experimentally altered in order to return to a prison they nearly died being expelled from not twenty-four hours prior? But he's underestimated our loyalty to the people inside The City.

"We couldn't ask any of you to do that," Doctor Gill protests. "When it's time, we have trained SDRT members who will be prepared to enter Ten. There are a few more tests I need to complete first. And, as General Rockshire pointed out, we need to make sure we can make the most of the operation. When we go in, we must have a way to deactivate the central computer while we're there. We're close, but not quite ready. Be patient. I promise, we're going to get your families out. I just don't want to risk doing this wrong and losing the best opportunity we may ever have. After we make a brief stop in Blue Haven, we'll be returning to Base Camp where the SDRT is headquartered. There, we'll be able to get a better sense of where things stand."

I can't say I like her answer, but it's hard to argue with. Patience has never been my strong suit, but I don't have any choice right now other than to trust Doctor Gill and the SDRT.

The floor of the hoverplane shifts gently forward.

"Looks like we're about to land in Blue Haven," General Rockshire announces. "As long as we're here, you might as well see it for yourselves. Follow me."

CHAPTER 6

The plane lands on a large paved field—smooth and well maintained like the streets of the Flame. I gather with the other refugees near the door, waiting for our escort to arrive. Gar and Kamella have taken a break from their games, and he clings to her side, eyes darting around nervously as we wait to disembark.

Near the door to exit the hoverplane, I take note of a glass box filled with dive bands. Even though I've used them once to bring me up to the hoverplane, I shudder at the thought of leaping while airborne with nothing but the bands and the promise they'll take me safely to the ground. Fortunately, the entire plane rests on solid ground, so dive bands won't be necessary.

Finally, Tella enters with an excited smile. "I get to be the one to show you around," she says. "Oh, and I found this for you, Kamella." She holds out a simple blue hat.

Kamella's eyes light up as she accepts the gift. "Thank you," she says, gathering up her unsightly hair and tucking it under the hat. With it on her head, no one could ever guess she'd recently sustained severe burns. "How do I look?" she asks Vander.

"Beautiful, as always," he says, helping her tuck a stray

lock into place and letting his hand linger against her cheek.

"Are you ready?" asks Tella. "You're going to love Blue Haven."

She presses a red button on the wall, and the door slides open. The roaring sound of the engines fills the room. Bright sunlight streams through the opening, and the scent of something floral and fresh assaults my nostrils.

"What's that smell?" I ask, slightly panicked. The scent is pleasant, but I'm not about to walk out into a new kind of Mind Mist.

I notice from the corner of my eyes that I'm not the only one alarmed. Vander and Kamella stiffen, and Shawny covers Quinn's face with a blanket and retreats from the door.

"I never thought I'd see people more paranoid than Toren," I hear Aiken whisper to Mara, and the two of them snicker.

"It's just the blossoms on the trees," Tella assures us. She descends the steps to the ground and points to the trees lining the streets nearby. They're vibrant and green, and their branches hang heavy with tiny clusters of white flowers. She inhales deeply. "Mmm, I've missed that scent. That's the smell of home."

Keaton saunters down the steps after her, followed closely by the people from Twelve.

"You're right, it does smell great," says Ty appreciatively, and bounds down the steps after them.

The hoverplane cuts its engines, and in the quiet left behind I can think more clearly. Slowly, I accept that it probably is just the aroma of flowers, and I follow, with Vander, Kamella, and Shawny right behind.

Tella pushes up her sleeve, revealing an implanted silver rectangle just like the one General Rockshire has. She taps it and says, "A car will be here in a moment to pick up Keaton and the boy, unless anyone else has decided to stay."

We all shake our heads.

"That's what I thought," she says. "Once they've been picked up to be taken to Integration Services, I'll show the rest of you around the city."

"What's that?" asks Keaton.

"Integration Services is responsible for integrating new arrivals into Blue Haven. They'll get you set up with a place to live and access to anything you need. And they'll place him with an adoptive family to care for him." Tella points to Gar, who has taken hold of both Kamella's and my hand as we walk across the wide concrete landing zone.

Less than a minute passes before a sleek, silver car pulls up in front of us.

"Thanks for everything," says Keaton, climbing inside.

"Here you are, my friend," Tella says to Gar. "Get inside."

He stares back with round, worried eyes.

"Come on," Kamella coaxes, leading him to the car. She bends down to hug him, and then lifts him onto the seat next to Keaton.

"Ahhh!" Gar cries. He leaps from the car and runs to me, wrapping both arms around me like a vise.

The poor child has no idea what's happening or what comes next. I wish I could do something for him—reassure him somehow—but at the moment, I'm nearly as uncertain about my own future.

I pick him up in my arms and hold him. "It's okay, it's okay," I chant into his ear.

Even though he doesn't understand the words, my soothing tone calms him, and he relaxes. His body is so lean, his bones pronounced. Food probably hasn't been a very predictable surety in his life up until this point.

Seeing the struggle we're having, Keaton exits the car and comes over to us. "I'll take him," he offers, holding out his arms.

I pass Gar's fragile form over, and he flails and cries and reaches out for me.

Though this boy has light hair, amber eyes, a long face, and looks nothing like my brother Whyle, in that moment of trust and concern, he reminds me so much of him that I have to look away so I don't race forward, grab him up in a hug, and make promises I can't keep. It's a good thing he's here, where things like food won't be a problem anymore. He'll see that soon enough.

I take a deep breath and look away as Keaton carries him into the car and they drive away. Heart aching, I shut my eyes, trying to avoid images of this boy that will haunt my dreams in days and years to come. I hope they'll find him a good family that will love him and treat him well. I hope that someday he'll get over the trauma this day must be inflicting on him.

"They'll take care of him," Tella promises, and starts walking.

I sigh and turn to follow her. That's when I finally begin to notice where we are. I've never seen anything like these towering buildings, twenty or more floors high. And enough cars zooming through the streets to carry thousands of people. Everyone we see appears healthy and well fed, with clean clothes and smiling faces. Blue Haven makes the grandeur of the Flame look pathetic in comparison. There's no question that Gar will have more here than he's ever had out in the wilderness with his crumbling, crippled parents, scrounging just to survive.

"This way," says Tella, leading us down a wide, perfectly paved sidewalk, lined with the fragrant flowering trees.

"So tell me," says Toren, pressing his way right through the middle of Vander and Kamella, forcing them to let go of each other's hands so he can reach the lead spot right next to Tella. "How'd this city get built up so fast? It seems pretty impressive to be just a few years' work of refugees and survivors."

I see what he means. Blue Haven is stunning. Looking around, you'd never guess the world beyond this city's borders is decimated and nearly deserted. Maybe Commander Elben wasn't exaggerating about what a perfect place they've created here. A part of me does want to stay, but not without Whyle, my parents, and Eason. This will never be my home until I've saved them and brought them back with me.

"We didn't build this city. We just had to fix it up a bit and get power back to it," says Tella. "It was once called Omaha, and it's pretty close to the center of the continent, which made it an ideal gathering place."

"How far away is your Base Camp?" I ask.

"Not far, just past the borders of a place that used to be called Colorado. We can fly there in a few hours. In fact, we'll pass right by Safe Dome Ten on our way."

"General Rockshire said everyone here is free to leave whenever they want," I say. "I notice a lot of people have cars. Do they drive between cities?"

"Oh, you can't drive anywhere outside of Blue Haven," she says.

"Why not?" Vander asks.

"No roads go in or out. It's essential to keep a tight control on transit, to make sure nothing like the Withers can ever happen again. That was how it spread so fast before—people from one area would travel between cities, completely unrestricted, carrying the disease from one group to the next before they even realized they were sick."

"So who decides who gets to go where?" Toren asks, clearly not buying her story about this setup being for people's own good. I have to admit, the isolated nature of Blue Haven is a little unsettling to me as well.

"No one decides," she replies. "Anyone can request a

transport by plane. As long as they clear a simple medical exam and go through decontamination, anyone is free to go."

That sets my misgivings at ease. It makes sense to try to learn from the disasters of the past. They'd be insane not to. Toren keeps shooting questions at her, looking for any inconsistencies in her words. I mostly tune his questions and Tella's responses out, breathing in the sweet, fresh air and enjoying the sunshine on my skin.

It takes me a while before I notice something—or a suspicious lack thereof. Since arriving, Ty hasn't said a single word. Not a single enthusiastic exclamation or compliment of the city has escaped his lips. He hasn't introduced himself to a single passerby as though they might be his new best friend. Very odd.

I look around and find him near the back of the group, behind Aiken and Mara. His eyes dart around, his expression an odd mixture of amazement and fear.

I let the others pass by so I can walk next to him. "Are you okay, Ty?"

He looks at me blankly and hesitates for a moment before he smiles. "Of course. Why wouldn't I be?"

I appraise him through a narrowed gaze, wondering if he's hiding something. But now his expression is nothing but serene and sincere, all traces of worry and confusion vanished. I remember vaguely what it was like being under the effects of the Mind Mist. There were moments when past thoughts and feelings of negativity and fear tried to break back into my awareness, but never quite could. The effects of the Mind Mist must be starting to wear off, leaving him with moments of deep confusion.

"Let me know if you…if you need someone to talk to. If you need help figuring out what's real," I say.

He shrugs, unconcerned. "Sure, I guess."

Suddenly, I walk straight into Kamella, knocking her hat right off her head.

"Hey," we both complain in unison but for different reasons.

She leans down to pick up her hat and put it back in place, covering her hair. That's when I see that Toren has hold of Tella's arm and has pulled her to a stop right in the middle of the street we're crossing.

"Now that's a print-worthy story in the making, if you ask me," says Toren, and I'm surprised he's managed to cram even more skepticism into his tone than usual.

"What do you mean?"

"Back in Sanctuary, I made it my job to expose secrets and lies. And when I figured out something we weren't supposed to know, I printed it and handed out hundreds of flyers for everyone to read."

"I see," Tella mutters.

"And that story about how no one is in charge here is about as phony a cover-up as I've ever heard. Give me a few days here, and I'll know who's really pulling the strings."

"There's really no government here?" Aiken asks.

I have to admit I'm just as curious, wondering what exactly was said when I wasn't listening.

Tella ushers us to the side of the road so we won't keep blocking traffic. "Let's go in here and eat some lunch while we talk." She leads us to a nearby building, a pretty little one-story box in the midst of so many towers. It's painted blue and yellow with a flashing sign that reads: *Café*.

"What's a kayf?" Kamella asks.

"Café," Tella corrects. "It's a place to eat."

When we approach, the tall glass doors slide open automatically. We enter a large, warmly lit, tiled space. Tables are scattered throughout the room—small cozy nooks for two, long tables and benches for a dozen, and everything in between. Only about a quarter of the tables are occupied. We follow Tella to a machine near the entrance, where two people stand in line. I don't think I've ever seen an eating area so empty at mealtime—not in the Smoke, the Flame, the Ash, and certainly not on the hoverplane.

"Where is everyone?" I ask. There's not nearly enough space in here to seat everyone we saw outside, even if food were served around the clock.

"Oh, there're lots of places to eat," Tella says. "And a lot of people just choose to eat at home. Everyone has one of these." She steps up to the machine.

"What is it?" Ty asks, his eyes wide.

"It's a Requisition Machine, or ReqMac for short," she says. "You can get whatever you need from machines like this. This one's specifically for food, but there are others that make clothes and supplies. Basically anything you need."

"How does it make it?" I ask.

Mara steps forward. "It's pretty simple," she says, running an admiring hand along the machine's smooth metal surface. "It's just stocked with all the basic elements, and when you select something, it assembles it," she explains. "It's a little more complicated than that, but that's the basic idea. But that's why each machine just makes certain types of things. It decreases how many components need to be stocked. Am I right?"

Tella raises her eyebrows in surprise. "Yeah, that's right. How did you know?"

"We have something pretty similar in Sanctuary. And, I don't know, it just seems pretty obvious," Mara says with a shrug.

"One time when we were younger, Mara reprogrammed our food dispenser to change our vegetables into ice cream," Aiken says with a fond smile, as though remembering a precious moment.

"You did that?" Vander asks Mara, his expression a mixture of admiration and skepticism.

"Yeah, I—" Mara begins, but Aiken cuts her off.

"No, not… Ugh…never mind," he says with a wearied sigh.

Mara's face shifts into a pout, and neither of them says another word.

"All right then," Tella says with a clap of her hands, breaking through the strange tension that's just developed. "Who's hungry?" She touches the screen and scrolls through what appear to be hundreds of options. "Just choose what you want to eat, and it'll come out here." She indicates a covered opening around the side of the machine.

Vander is the first to step forward, and appears to be looking for something specific as he scans through the options. Finally he taps the screen, and seconds later, the decadent scent of hot bacon wafts through the air. He steps to the side and opens the flap on the ReqMac to reveal a steaming hot plate piled with bacon and potatoes.

"Yes!" he exclaims, bringing the plate up to his nose and inhaling deeply.

"Can I try?" Kamella asks.

"Of course," Tella encourages. "What would you like?"

"My mom used to talk about something called shrimp. Do you have that?"

I laugh, figuring a food called shrimp must have been a product of Mind Mist-induced delirium. It can't possibly be a real thing. But I'm quickly proven wrong when a plate of small, creepy-looking, pink-and-white fish appear, and as she carries it past me, I'm taken aback by a strange odor I've never experienced before.

Next, Shawny gets a bowl of some kind of chunky stew that smells delicious.

"And how about you, Emery?" Tella asks.

I don't hesitate or consider. "Chocolate," I say, my mouth watering at the memory of the delicious, dark square Eason gave me on our last morning together.

"What kind?" Tella proceeds to show me a list of no less than twenty ways I can have chocolate prepared: dark, milk, white, cake, ice cream, fudge, pie, shake. I have no idea what most of those things are.

"I don't know. What's your favorite?"

She scans through the list, considering, and then chooses something called a molten fudge cake. I retrieve it from the ReqMac and pinch off a few crumbs to try. The overwhelming sensation of pure deliciousness is so profound that my eyes start to water.

"Blazes, that's good," I exclaim.

I join the others at a large table they've chosen for us. I fill my mouth with another bite and close my eyes, allowing myself to indulge in a fantasy for just a moment—one where I bring Eason here, and I get to be the one to introduce him to something more amazing than he's ever tasted before. I picture the look of surprise and pleasure on his perfect face and the way his blue eyes light up as they gaze back into mine. But I don't let my imagination settle into the daydream because, as much as it thrills and comforts me, it's the kind of thought that will torture me later if it's never able to transcend imagination into reality.

In the few short minutes it takes the rest of the group to select their own meals—all of them choosing foods I don't recognize—Vander, Kamella, and I have all cleaned our plates. Shawny is doing her best to feed herself and Quinn at the same time. It's slowing her down, but she doesn't seem to mind.

Toren and Tella join us at our table, but Aiken and Mara choose to sit alone at a smaller table across the room even though there are plenty of seats with us. I watch them lean in and talk in a conspiratorial way. I can't figure them out. They seem to be close, but they don't act anything like Vander and Kamella. Mara might love Aiken, but I don't think he feels the same way. Still, he clearly has some kind of affection for her—even though the two of them can't seem to agree whether or not her name actually is Mara. The whole situation is very strange. I wonder if there's something about Twelve I don't know, a piece of the puzzle I'm not seeing.

Fortunately, whatever's going on with them really isn't my problem, and I certainly have enough of my own to worry about. As much as I'd like to see all the Safe Domes freed, my only real concern is getting back to The City and rescuing Eason and my family. Someone else can figure out the rest of it.

"So what were you saying about there being no government?" Vander says, bringing us back to our earlier conversation.

"There's not a lot more to say about it," says Tella. "There's no government. Governments are inherently flawed because they're run by a few people who can never truly understand and consider the needs of every individual. Here, everyone has equal say and authority."

"So how does that work?" I ask. "If someone does something wrong, anyone can just... arrest them or something?"

"Kind of, but not exactly. Everyone is implanted with one of these." Tella rolls up her sleeve to reveal the silver rectangle on her forearm. "It's a city interface."

"Wow!" exclaims Ty.

Toren huffs.

I can't help wondering if this is just a new upgrade to the intercuffs that control people in The City.

"This connects to Blue Haven's main computer," Tella explains.

"So you've got your own version of Ember here," Vander scoffs.

I shudder and suddenly want nothing more than to run away and escape this place.

"No, not at all. Blue Haven's computer isn't in charge of us; it simply connects us. It doesn't create or impose rules. It's more like a calculator tallying votes, and a messenger sending signals. We all have equal say in what happens, and equal authority to stop injustice from occurring to ourselves and to others. And it works. There's no crime in Blue Haven. There's no reason to deal unfairly with each other when you have everything you could ever need, and you know you're safe. Who are you going to fight when no one has control over your life except you?"

We're silent for a moment, considering what she's said.

"Hmm. Sounds awfully suspicious to me," Toren finally says.

Tella laughs. "Suit yourself, but I could introduce you

to dozens of people from Twelve who have been living here quite happily for some time. I'm sure you know most of them."

"I'll judge that for myself," he retorts, his mouth half-full of something slimy and red.

"So what else should we know about Blue Haven?" asks Kamella.

Tella gives her an appreciative smile, grateful for a shift in the conversation. She starts talking about how Blue Haven's society is set up. "Kids go to school until they're sixteen. Then they make a choice about what job they want. Depending on what they choose, they go into a specialized training program."

"So anyone can choose anything they want?" I ask, hardly able to fathom what kind of a society that would create. In The City, all our assignments came from the Council—or rather, the computer.

"What if they aren't any good at what they choose?" Vander asks.

"That's why we train them." She says it as though anyone can be good at anything with the proper instruction. Could that possibly be true? Or maybe people don't choose things they aren't good at. I think of Petra, my wonderfully talented maid during my time in the Burning. Her passions and abilities didn't relate to cleaning. Here in Blue Haven, she could be a hair stylist or fashion designer or whatever she chose. And she would be fabulous at her work and so much happier.

But what would I choose to do if I could do anything?

Certainly not building repair or window cleaning—both things I've done plenty of back home. I can name things I don't want to do, but what do I want to do? Up until now, life has just been about doing whatever it took to survive—completing my assignments in the Smoke, passing the Burning, working on the farm. The idea that I could decide my own path hasn't ever occurred to me, and I'm not quite sure how to handle it.

Thankfully, I don't have to decide now. I'm not even staying here in Blue Haven—not yet. Before anything here matters for me, I have a score to settle with Ember and people to save.

A quiet chime sounds from Tella's city interface. She looks down and reads something displayed there. "You'll have to excuse me for a moment," she says, getting to her feet. We start to rise as well, but she motions for us to stay. "I just have to take care of something, and I'll be back for you soon. Please, just wait here. Help yourselves to more food if you'd like."

We sit back down as she exits the café. I can see out the window that she's heading back in the direction of the hoverplane, but there's an enormous building blocking our view of the landing zone from here.

A few minutes pass, and I decide to take her up on her offer for more food, not because I'm still hungry, but just because it's so delicious. Just a few days ago, I never would have dreamed there would come a time in my life when food would be abundant and delicious and something you could consume for the simple pleasure of it. I'm not exactly sure if I could get used to living here, but I'm beginning to look forward to giving it a try.

"Something's not right about this," Toren murmurs.

"How so?" Kamella asks, since he's clearly anxious to say more.

But before he gets the chance to explain, or I get a chance to fill my stomach with more food, Mara's head snaps up and she whispers something to Aiken.

He jumps to his feet and yells, "They're leaving without us!" And he and Mara take off running.

CHAPTER 7

The rest of us look around in stunned surprise for a moment, wondering how they could possibly know that. We can't even see the hoverplane from here. But it only takes a couple seconds for us to all realize it doesn't matter how they know. If there's any chance it's true, we'd better make a run for it.

We draw stares from the other café patrons as we frantically scramble to our feet. I'm the first to reach the exit, and have to slow my pace to allow time for the automatic glass door to slide open. But as soon as I'm outside, I take off at a full sprint. Now that my leg is healed I can really run again, and it feels great.

"Race you!" yells Ty as he passes Kamella and Shawny.

Vander and Ty are the only ones keeping up with me. Aiken and Mara, with their head start, are already rounding the next corner. Kamella isn't much of a runner and neither is Toren, it turns out. And Shawny has a baby in her arms slowing her down.

I've only traversed half the distance back to the hoverplane when I hear the tremendous roar of the engines sputtering to life.

"They're really leaving us!" I shout in aggravation,

wondering how Mara and Aiken could possibly have known.

I reach the landing zone and see that the door to the hoverplane is still open. I increase my pace, focusing all my strength and energy on the single goal of reaching that door before it closes. But it's not enough, and I'm still too far away when the door starts to close. At the last moment, Aiken and Mara manage to slip through the shrinking opening.

"No!" I shout, still running with everything I have.

Aiken catches sight of us, and then the door closes, and the steps leading up to it retract underneath the belly of the plane. There's a moment when it appears we've missed our chance, and then the door reopens. Aiken stands there waving his arms to us and shouting something I can't hear.

Quickly, I close the remaining distance and leap up, grabbing the edge and pulling myself up through the doorway onto the plane.

Vander makes it in next, and then Ty. Toren is a ways back, followed by Kamella, and I can't even see Shawny and the baby from here.

The hoverplane starts to roll slowly down the runway.

"Hurry!" Vander yells.

"They aren't going to make it!" I cry.

"We have to close the door before we ascend," yells Aiken.

As though on cue, the hoverplane's speed increases, and it loses contact with the ground, rising slowly but steadily.

"Kamella!" Vander screams.

In a sudden flurry of motion, Vander leaps through the open door, dropping several feet back to the ground. He hits the pavement and rolls several times before sliding to a stop.

I stand there frozen in shock. I never would have thought Vander would choose anyone over his twin brother, but I guess Kamella means more to him than I had realized.

Aiken pulls me away from the door's opening and slams his fist against the red button, closing the door before any of us tumble to our deaths.

Heart racing, muscles shaking with adrenaline, I turn to find Mara with her back against the far wall. Her eyes are wide and she's running her hands furiously through her flowing blond hair. Ty's standing in the middle of the space, looking intermittently elated and confused.

As soon as my legs stop shaking, I step toward the door that leads to the interior of the hoverplane.

"Where are you going?" Aiken whispers, holding out a hand to stop me.

I brush him away. "I'm going to go give Elben and Rockshire a piece of my mind and make them go back for the others."

"Hold on," says Aiken. "They don't know we're on board. They could just as easily turn around and kick the four of us off."

I pause. "What makes you think they don't know

we're here?"

"Simple. They took off with the door still open, and no one is here to meet us," he says. "As far as I can tell, neither of those things are protocol for this situation. So I think it's pretty safe to assume they don't know we made it on board or that I reopened the door."

"So what do you suggest we do?" I ask.

"We should wait here until we reach Base Camp. At that point, we'll have to reveal ourselves if we want food or to have any hope of being included in their plans. But once we're there, it probably won't be worth the trouble of taking us back, and they might just keep their promise to let us stay and help, after all."

I start to pace back and forth across the small space, thinking through the situation. There's no chance we can go back for the others now, and they're probably plenty safe in Blue Haven, anyway. But that means it's up to the four of us to make sure our families are rescued—including Van and Shawny's kids, and Kamella's parents. My list of responsibilities just keeps growing.

Aiken's probably right about the SDRT not realizing we're here. But before I decide what to do next, I need some answers. "Fine, we'll wait here," I say. "But while we do, I want to know exactly how you knew they were about to leave us?"

Aiken and Mara lock eyes for a moment, sharing another wordless exchange.

"All right," Aiken finally says. "But you might want to sit down. There are things you don't know about Mara and Sanctuary."

I settle on the floor with my back leaning against the wall, and Ty eagerly sits down next to me. Aiken sighs and takes a seat next to Mara.

"Are you sure we should tell them?" she whispers, as though she thinks we can't hear.

"Yes," says Aiken. "We need allies, and they're in the same situation we are—more or less. I think we can trust them." He turns to us. "I'm not sure exactly how to explain this so it doesn't sound crazy," he hedges.

"Trust me, I've dealt with my fair share of crazy lately," I say. "All I want is the truth."

"Sanctuary is a paradise," says Mara. "Everything is perfect, and runs on clear and neat systems."

"Everything is not perfect," Aiken mutters, clearly annoyed, and her lower lip quivers as though she's fighting not to cry—again. To me he says, "Sanctuary seems perfect because we have plenty of food and nice things. Everyone has a Duty assigned to them and is well cared for. But at some point, the city started replacing its citizens with robot copies of themselves."

I have to admit, that's not what I was expecting to hear.

"Wow! Your own robot twin?" Ty says, and I'm not entirely sure if he finds the idea scary or he's wishing he had a robot replica of himself to do pranks with.

"What do you mean 'replacing?'" I ask.

"A few weeks ago, the Governor announced that they would begin sending people out of Sanctuary to explore and see what was happening in the world outside. Mara has never been happy in Sanctuary. She signed up, and I followed her," Aiken explains.

I look at Mara, who seems to have pulled herself back together. "Really? But you speak so highly of Sanctuary now," I say, surprised.

"Well, you see…" Mara trails off, pulling at a lock of hair nervously.

"I keep telling you all: that's not Mara," says Aiken. "That's what I'm trying to explain. That is the robot that replaced Mara."

"Is this true?" I ask the girl, finding it difficult to believe she isn't entirely human.

She sighs heavily and looks at the ground. "Yes," she finally admits morosely.

"That's why you didn't want the doctors to scan her?" I guess, pieces of the puzzle starting to click into place.

Aiken nods.

"So they just went around switching people with robot twins?" I say, trying to figure out how that could work without anyone noticing.

"They used the Explorer Program as an excuse to pair us up with partners," Aiken explains. "We were told our partner was evaluating whether or not we would be chosen to be explorers, but really they were learning absolutely everything about us. Once they were able to essentially become us, the real people were secretly expelled from the Safe Dome. Our robot counterparts' appearance was changed to be a perfect match, and the robots took over our identities. Our families were told we weren't chosen to leave Sanctuary after all. Only those people whose robot counterparts were not able to get a good enough read on them to replicate them will seem to have actually left the Safe Dome."

"So how is this Mara here?" I ask. "Shouldn't she still be in Sanctuary and the real Mara be here with you?"

"The real Mara discovered the truth just before they came for her to send her away. She thought they were going to kill all of us, so she managed to switch places with her robot copy," he explains.

"How did she do that?" I ask, amazed.

"Mara is basically a genius when it comes to technology—which is one of the reasons she's never really fit in at Sanctuary. She always sees ways things could be different or unique ways to solve problems. She realized the robots' main purpose was to preserve the human ideas and personalities while removing irrationality and unpredictability. She did something to her Mara-bot to enhance her emotionality. It only took about two seconds for the highly agitated and distraught robot to be mistaken for a human and sent with the group being expelled. She even fooled me for a few days. But the real Mara is now trapped in Sanctuary, pretending to be her own robot copy." As he talks about Mara—the real Mara—his voice is heavy with admiration and longing and fear.

I'm amazed at how different each of the Safe Domes appears to be. The City, Sanctuary, and Reprieve all have very different systems. But each is just another brand of awful.

Given this information, everything makes sense, from the way Aiken and this Mara seem to have a strained but oddly affectionate relationship, to the dedication Aiken has to getting back to Sanctuary—to his love—which this Mara doesn't quite share.

"Why don't you call this Mara robot something else?" I ask. "It would save a lot of confusion."

"Before she took on Mara's identity she was called Darla, but she cries every time I call her that now," Aiken explains with a grimace.

"You might not understand it, but in my own way I *am* Mara now," she says sheepishly. "It's not fair for you to tell me I can't be who I am."

"And because Mara—human Mara—is in love with Aiken, you…" I let the words trail off, my implication clear.

Mara's mouth turns down into a mournful frown. She turns a longing gaze on Aiken and nods.

He shrugs. "Drives me crazy, but what am I supposed to do?"

"Okay," I say with a shrug. I guess I'm not the only one with a complicated love life around here. "Maybe the real Mara will just admit she's a human, and they'll expel her from Sanctuary after all," I say encouragingly. "Wouldn't that be as good a solution as any? Just get all the humans out and the robots can have Twelve. Problem solved."

"It's not that simple," says Mara. "You see, prototypes—or rather, humans—who aren't able to be replicated by a robot are eliminated."

"You mean *killed*?" I say.

She nods. "Anyone who's too unpredictable or has brain patterns that don't fit the standard models can't be duplicated. Honestly, I only barely managed to figure Mara out in time. She's a…unique person. The Leader sees them as a threat, not only to Sanctuary, but to all of humanity. To try and protect them from inflicting harm on others, he has decided it's necessary to deactivate them."

"And you think that's what he would do to the real Mara if he discovered what she's done?"

Mara nods. "Almost certainly."

"And the Leader, is that your governor?" I ask.

"No, although Governor Hydes has been replaced by a bot," Mara says. "The leader of the robots was the first robot in Sanctuary, the one all the others were modeled after. His name is Maxel, and as far as most people know, he's the school teacher."

"But here's the strange thing about that," Aiken says. "Maxel is the spitting image of Commander Elben—the Architect."

"Weird," Ty mutters. "I knew that guy was tricky."

I recall the way Aiken and Mara reacted in the conference room when they first met him. "Are you saying Elben was in Sanctuary, and he was the first one replaced by a robot?"

Aiken shrugs. "I'm not sure. But I heard someone call him Maxton, so think about that. His name is Maxton Elben… Max El… Maxel. It has to be related to him somehow. And if he's the Architect who created the Safe Domes, then he must have been the one who created the original robot in Sanctuary. I guess it makes sense he would make it look like him, as arrogant as he is."

I can't argue about Elben's arrogance. But was it really his plan all along to have robots replace the people of Sanctuary and kill the ones they couldn't replace? How does that help protect people against the Withers?

"Maybe this Maxel robot is Sanctuary's computer and it got out of control and went rogue the same way the rest of them did," I surmise. "It doesn't mean Elben did it on purpose."

"Mara—human Mara—says she's found the central computer, and it's located in the Governor's House. So it can't be Maxel," says Mara.

"She told you that before you left Sanctuary?" I ask.

"No, she told me that today."

"But I thought you all left Sanctuary several days ago," I say, confused.

"Five days ago," Aiken confirms.

My pulse quickens. "You mean you're able to communicate with her now?" I say, certain this is important even if I can't say exactly how just yet.

"Yes, she opened up a communication link with me when she switched places with me so she could find out what happened to the prototypes… I mean humans. It took me a few days to discover the connection, but we've been in contact since before the SDRT picked us up."

"I think Mara's a lot more likely to find a way to bring down the Safe Domes than that idiot Architect is," Aiken mutters.

"How could she do that?" I ask.

"It's all about my connection to the central computer," says Mara. "It turns out that all the robots are connected to the central computer. It's an incredibly complex system, and highly protected. The best we've figured out so far is a way to basically stun it for several minutes. It's similar to what she did to me when she switched places, but on a much bigger scale."

"Would that deactivate the barrier field, too?" I ask.

"I think so," says Mara.

"So why doesn't the real Mara do it and get out?" I ask.

"I tried to convince her to do just that," Aiken says. "But it wouldn't be nearly enough time to get all the other humans out, and she won't leave them behind."

"But what you may be interested to know," says Mara-bot, "is that I've discovered my connection to Sanctuary's main computer actually ties me into every Safe Dome's computer."

"You're connected to Ember?" I shout in elation, then cover my mouth and listen in case my outburst has drawn the attention of anyone in the hallway nearby. We wait in anxious silence for a beat, but no one comes.

"Can you deactivate the others, too?" I whisper.

She shakes her head. "I can feel the connection, but I can't break through the protective shielding that surrounds it. Most likely, the Wall of Fire protects it from unwanted connections. But if I could get a transmitter inside that layer, I'd have access."

She pulls a small silver sphere from the bag she carries at her waist and tosses it in the air with a mischievous grin—Eason's transmitter.

"That transmitter is broken," I say, my elevated hopes quickly waning.

"Was," says Mara. "It was broken. It's not anymore."

"You fixed it?" I ask in amazement.

"I fixed it," she confirms. "So to answer your original question: this is how I picked up the message that they were preparing for takeoff without us."

"That was so wrong of them," Ty mutters in a rare moment of near-lucidity—a sign the Mind Mist is slowly losing its grip on him.

"I didn't know it could be used to listen to transmissions," I admit. The only sound I've ever heard it make is a high-pitched beep when Vander and I activated it in the Ash in hopes of dissolving the barrier field.

"Here, I'll show you," she says. "It'll probably just pick up static right now, but if there are any signals being sent nearby, we should be able to listen in."

She twists the sphere in ways I didn't know it could or should move, and soon sound is streaming from the device. But it's not crackling, meaningless static, and the sound sends chills through my veins, as though my blood has turned to ice.

CHAPTER 8

I've only heard this voice once before, but I would recognize it anywhere. Though the signal is broken and choppy, the cold, inhuman woman's voice can be none other than Ember. We've missed the beginning, and I strain to keep up and decipher what's being said.

"…the Smoke does not return to their assignments by dawn, there will be fatalities, beginning with Eason Crandell."

In that instant, I simultaneously process two important facts: Eason must still be alive, and Eason's life is now being used as Ember's bargaining chip.

I understand why she would blame him for the precarious situation The City is now in. He's the one who built the transmitters. In a way, it's because of him that the Ash rebelled and the SDRT is now closing in on a way to deactivate the Safe Dome.

Even so, I don't understand why she hasn't just expelled or killed him already. I shudder at the thought, but if I'm being rational, it's true. There's no reason for her to keep him at this point unless she thinks she can use him somehow. And that means she believes Eason has some special value, more so than any other random citizen she could have threatened.

But why?

"So what does all of that mean?" Aiken asks, confused, but realizing it clearly means something to me. "What was that first bit about smoke?"

"The Smoke is the outer rim of The City," Ty explains with perfect clarity, drawing a surprised gaze from everyone in the room. "It sounded like they've abandoned their work assignments. That's probably the work of the Resistance." Then his face scrunches in concentration, as through he's fighting to remain clear-headed and the effort is painful.

A cold sweat dampens my palms and forehead, my ears ring, and everything feels too close and too loud, even though no one is speaking or moving. In desperation, I grip Ty by his shirt. "You have to tell the Resistance to stop this!" I say. "Mara can transmit the message, but we need their secret code so Ember won't understand it, and so they'll trust us."

He squints and rubs his temples. "I... I think I remember the code. We could tell them, but I doubt it'll make a difference."

"Why?"

"Because for years, this fight is what they've been preparing for," he says.

"That thing is going to kill Eason *tomorrow* if we don't do something now. We can't wait for the SDRT to figure this out," I say with resolve, the first hints of a plan starting to form in my mind.

"Who's Eason?" Mara asks.

I direct my response to Aiken. "Eason is my Mara," I say, and I can see in his eyes that he understands perfectly how that transmission just changed everything and sealed my fate. There is nothing I won't do to save him now.

I pace the small room, trying to work out what I'm going to do next. I have to find a way to get Eason out of Ember's reach before she can hurt him any more than she most certainly already has.

Going to Commander Elben or General Rockshire with this new information won't do any good. Doctor Gill already made it clear they aren't prepared to do a human test of DS10 for several weeks. By then, I might not have anything or anyone left to live for. Which makes my decision relatively simple: I'd rather die now for the people I love than live for nothing later.

In a flurry of motion, I rush to the exterior door and slam my palm against the red button that opens it to the sky. The door begins to retract, filling the room with a sound like a hundred recycling machines running all at once.

"What are you doing?" Aiken demands, ripping me away from the opening.

"Let me go," I protest, twisting out of his grip and racing back to the door.

It only takes one glance to see exactly what I was hoping for. Tella said we'd pass right by The City on our way to Base Camp. If we picked up that signal, it must mean we're close. As I peer out, I see that we're currently flying over the mountain where I was attacked—where we rescued Gar. The inferno that surrounds The City still burns. That will be tricky to contend with, but I'll find a way. I just need to be ready when the plane passes as near to The City as possible. I can't waste hours or days trekking back and risk running into more Roamers.

Without a word, I hit the button to seal the door again before the plane shifts and any of us are accidentally tossed out. Then I turn and start talking. "Mara, are you sure you can deactivate the computer if we get that transmitter inside the Wall of Fire?"

"Yes, I believe so. Though the closer we can get it to the computer, the stronger the signal. It won't be permanent, though. The most I could guarantee is about thirty minutes," she says.

"That'll have to do," I say. "Ty, I need you to give Mara a coded message. Alert the Resistance that the barrier field will be down for a limited time. Give them a chance to get as many people out as possible."

"What about the real fire outside?" Ty asks, eyes wide.

"They'll have to find a way to deal with that," is all I can say. "Maybe they can gather heat shields from the metal recycling plants. It should help, at least." I step to the door that leads to the interior of the plane. "Can you send the message now?"

"As soon as Ty has it ready," Mara confirms.

"Ty, can you do it?" I demand.

"Um, I… I think so," says Ty, rubbing his forehead.

"Good. You've got about two minutes."

"What are you…" Aiken begins.

"They're about to know we're here," I mutter as I open the door. The instant I can squeeze through, I'm in the hallway and running straight for the Hospital Wing with a singular focus and goal. Several people exclaim and jump out of the way as I rush past, but I don't stop or apologize. I plan to be back in the launch room before word of our presence spreads.

"What?" several doctors exclaim at once as I burst into the brightly lit Hospital Wing.

My eyes dart around for the briefest second before landing on what I came for. Doctor Gill is sitting at a desk, and the black box containing the DNA shifting medication sits right in front of her. Fortunately, she's so startled by my sudden appearance that it doesn't occur to her what I might be after until it's too late. Before anyone reacts at all, I've already scooped up the box and sprinted back into the hallway.

On my way to the Hospital Wing I encountered only a few SDRT members, but now more are gathering. The people I pass are confused by the disturbance, but make no effort to detain me. Not until I'm nearly back to the launch room where Mara, Aiken, and Ty wait.

"Stop!" General Rockshire commands from a few paces away, running to catch up, but I'm faster.

Aiken has the door open for me. As soon I pass through he closes it, and Mara does something that seems to jam it, because none of General Rockshire's attempts to gain entry have any effect.

"Did you send the message?" I ask.

"Yes, but I can't be sure they got it," says Mara, her expression flustered.

I'm putting a lot of trust in this unstable robot, and I hope I don't end up regretting it. I just don't have any better options.

"I guess we'll just have to hope," I say as I slide dive bands, silver side out, onto my wrists and ankles. I'm glad I'm moving so fast I don't have time to really consider what I'm about to do.

"Are you sure about this?" asks Aiken.

"Positive," I reply, and open the door that leads to the vastness of the sky.

The City is close—as close as it's going to be. If I jump now, I should be able to keep it in my sights from wherever I land and hike back fairly quickly—as long I don't end up with a broken leg from the fall.

Clutching the black box to my chest, determined not to lose it no matter how terrifying the descent may be, I take a deep breath, bend my legs, and…

The door slams shut.

"No!" I scream, recovering my balance before I crash nose-first into metal. Desperately, I hit the red button to reopen it, but there's no effect.

Behind me, General Rockshire has still not managed to break through whatever Mara did to the door, but his voice booms from above. "Stop, Emery. You're not going anywhere with that."

I know it's only a matter of minutes before they find a

way in, and with every passing second we float farther and farther away from The City. There's one way—and one way only—that I can ensure they won't stop me. I rip open the box and take out the single syringe right here and now.

"Careful with that!" Doctor Gill's voice cries through the speakers. "It'll take me days to synthesize more if it's lost."

I grip the syringe in one fist and ram the needle straight through my clothes and into my thigh, compressing quickly on the plunger and emptying the entire contents into my body. I don't know if this is the proper method of administration, but it's not like anyone was likely to give me directions.

Then I take the small vial filled with Curosene and do the only thing I can to ensure they can't reverse what I've done and stop me. I throw it hard to the metal floor, and it shatters into tiny, wet shards. It doesn't matter; I know where I can get more once I'm back in The City.

"Let me go!" I holler. "It won't do anyone any good to keep me here now." I pound against the door again, but my arms feel weak. The walls and floor are shifting like they're made of sponge and won't hold their shape.

"Emery!" Aiken exclaims so loud I think my head is going to explode.

I cover my ears and sink to the ground.

"Emery, are you okay?" Mara asks, quieter but still too loud. She rests a hand on my shoulder, and it feels like dozens of teeth are biting into me. I try to pull away, but can't seem to move at all.

"We need the doctor," says Aiken. "Mara, open the door."

"No," I scream, but it comes out as an indecipherable moan because I can't make my mouth move the way it's supposed to.

Mara ignores me, maybe because she can't understand me, or maybe because she'll do absolutely anything Aiken asks of her. Either way, the door slides open.

Doctor Gill and her identical twin kneel at my side. "Emery, can you hear me?" they both say in unison, the sounds carrying an odd dissonance that bores into my skull.

"Yes," I try to say, but no sound comes out.

"Get her to the Hospital Wing!" the doctors command, and a man scoops me up and hauls my limp body down the hallway. I try to fight him, but my muscles just won't respond to my commands.

They set me down on a bed of hot coals, and I scream.

Doctor Gill has morphed into triplets now, and one of them begins slicing my throat while the others mirror her actions.

The world melts into an unrecognizable sludge until it ceases to exist at all.

CHAPTER 9

The big surprise when I wake up is that I'm still alive, and I seem to have recovered the use of my muscles. The Hospital Wing is empty except for Doctor Gill and one man who looks to be standing guard over me.

"Emery, can you hear me?" Doctor Gill asks when she sees me stir. All traces of her doppelgängers are gone.

"Yes," I say, and the sound comes out crisp and clear, much to my relief.

Tella peeks her head out from one of the patient rooms and waves. I scowl and turn away. I trusted her, and she abandoned us.

I tense and relax my muscles; I've regained full control and feel perfectly fine now. As though by reflex, I prepare to make a run back for the exit. Maybe we're still close enough to The City for me to find my way back by nightfall, but then I notice that my dive bands have been removed. I'm guessing it won't be so easy this time to get more, and the exit is still sealed, I'm sure. I let the impulse to escape pass.

I'll have to figure out another way. I assess my situation, looking for anything that might be helpful, but nothing really comes to mind.

It takes another minute for my mind to calm and focus, and then I remember Doctor Gill slicing my neck. Frantically, I feel for the cut, but there's nothing but a tiny needle prick. "What did you do to me?" I demand.

"I just gave you an injection to help your cells stabilize."

"You reversed it?" I ask in horror. "Was that Curosene?"

"No, you destroyed the only Curosene we had on board. We'll have to wait until we reach Base Camp to get more. What I gave you just helped your cells adjust to the transition. The process is very disorienting for the body."

"So I can still get through the barrier field?" I sit up too fast and dizziness overtakes me. I give it a second to pass before I get to my feet.

"Theoretically, yes," she confirms. "But it's out of the question. We're almost at Base Camp, and I'll reverse it immediately once we arrive."

"That's ridiculous!" I argue. "You need a test subject, and here I am, ready and willing. Send me in! There's no reason not to."

"I already told you, we need a plan of attack on the computer when we go in. We're just not ready."

"I may have a solution for that, too."

This draws a skeptical gaze. "How so?"

"Where are the others—Mara, Aiken, and Ty?"

"I think the general has them in a holding room to keep them from getting into any more trouble."

"Then get them. We need to talk to General Rockshire and Commander Elben."

"Commander Elben doesn't have time to meet with you," she says. "He already agreed with me that you'll receive Curosene as soon as we reach Base Camp. Then you'll stand trial for your crimes."

"What?" I stammer.

"Emery, you not only stowed away on board when you were supposed to remain in Blue Haven, but you stole vital research. The loss of the compound you injected will set this program back. If we're extremely lucky it will only be a matter of days, but it may be weeks or months for me to recreate what you wasted. I don't know how things are in Ten, but out here there are consequences for reckless, selfish, and dangerous actions."

"You all lied to us. We were promised we could stay until the Safe Domes were deactivated. Why tell us about your discovery at all if you just planned to ditch us?"

"At the time I didn't know that was the plan," she admits, her tone regretful. "I suppose General Rockshire thought that if you knew we had a plan, it would give you some peace of mind while you waited to be reunited with your families."

"Well, the only thing that'll give me peace of mind now is if you let me go. Give me a chance to rescue my family. I have information that I think Commander Elben will be interested in."

I start for the door, but the man standing guard steps in my path.

"You're not going anywhere," he says in a deep monotone. I wonder if he and General Rockshire get together and practice sounding utterly emotionless in high-stress situations, or if it just comes naturally to both of them.

I turn and search for Tella. Surely she'll help, but she's disappeared back into a room, leaving me to fend for myself.

"Please sit down, or I'll be forced to restrain you," the man says, as though he'd be equally satisfied with either option.

Defeated, I take a seat on the bed. From here, I can see the flames of The City receding into the distance, my only hope of rescuing Eason disappearing with them.

* * *

All at once, the door to the Hospital Wing bursts open and Commander Elben storms in. "What is this about a way to deactivate Ten?" he shouts. "Why do I have to hear this from a random crew member?"

Tella peeks her head out again just long enough for me to see her wink, and then she makes herself scarce. Probably a good idea. Whatever happens now, though, Tella has redeemed herself to me.

Doctor Gill rushes over in alarm. "Maxton, there wasn't anything to tell. The girl is clearly a thief and a liar. How could she possibly know how to deactivate the computer?"

"I do," I insist.

"So let's hear it," he says, his expression making it clear that if I don't deliver, I will pay for it.

"We need to talk to Mara," I say. "It involves her."

"That sniveling girl?" he asks with distaste.

"She's not who she appears to be," I say. "Trust me, this isn't something you've dealt with before." Then I remember what Aiken said about the first robot in Sanctuary being a replica of Commander Elben, and I think he probably has dealt with this before, but isn't aware that one of the robots is on the outside.

"Then let's go have a little chat," says Commander Elben. He turns and marches toward the door. No one moves. "Now!" he commands.

Doctor Gill and the guard jump into action. I get to my feet as well, and we all follow him out into the hallway. The guard grips my arm as we walk.

"I'm not going anywhere," I complain, pulling out of his grasp. He must realize there's no chance I can escape while we're hundreds of feet in the air, with the exit sealed and my dive bands removed, so he lets me walk on my own.

"General, gather the other refugees and meet us in the conference room," Elben says into his city interface. It strikes me as odd that the Blue Haven interface seems to work anywhere. How can the computer's range be so large? But it's of little consequence to me now, so I quickly put it from my mind.

"Have a seat," my guard instructs when we enter the

conference room.

It's difficult to believe that it was just this morning I sat here with all the others—most of whom are back in Blue Haven now. I'm surprised to find how much I wish Vander were here with me. We've been through so much together over the past week, and I hadn't realized how much I'd come to rely on him until now, when he's gone. But the fact that he's not here is all the more reason to see this through—not just for Whyle and Eason, but for Van.

A few tense minutes tick by while we wait. Finally, General Rockshire enters, followed by Mara, Aiken, and Ty.

"All right, let's hear it," growls Commander Elben. "And I'd better be utterly amazed by your plan, considering the cost it's already incurred."

"We can get people out of Ten now," I begin. "If you let me go into The City, I know how to get past the Wall of Fire. There are secret tunnels that I know about. I can get to the Council Building where the computer is."

"And what good will that do, exactly?" Elben asks, but I can tell he's listening.

"I'll take a transmitter with me, and once it's placed near the computer's main systems, Mara can shut it down."

All eyes turn to the quivering girl who looks so human that, for a moment, I have to doubt if anything she and Aiken told me is actually true.

"And how can you do that?" asks General Rockshire.

"I… Well, you see…" she stammers.

"She's a robot," I blurt out.

This elicits mixed reactions, everything from surprise to laughter. But Commander Elben's face stays frozen, and I know he believes me, and he also knows exactly what that means.

"Tell them what you told me," I say to Mara and Aiken. There's no point in secrets now.

Reluctantly, Aiken recounts the entire sequence of events that led to them being expelled from Twelve. "Mara has found that she has a connection not only to the main computer in Sanctuary, but to all the computers. The one in Ten is shielded by that Wall of Fire thing, but with a transmitter inside, she could connect to it."

"Is this true?" Commander Elben asks Mara.

She nods.

"And you can use this connection to deactivate it?" he demands. His expression is unreadable, which is strange. I would think he'd be elated at the prospect that the mistakes he made—and has spent nearly a decade trying to correct—could finally be at an end-point. But maybe he's just being cautious, considering there are no guarantees at this point.

"I don't think I can shut it down for good," she admits. "But I should be able to stun it. It would take about thirty minutes for it to reset. That should also deactivate the barrier field for that same interval. With proper warning, you could get a lot of people out."

At this, Commander Elben finally smiles. "Excellent.

Sounds like a plan. Let's give it a go," he says with a clap of his hands.

"Can I point out that warning the people is the same as warning Ember?" says General Rockshire.

"Not with Ty," I say, smiling. "Ty was part of a secret group of resisters. He can send a coded message that only the Resistance will be able to decipher."

"We already sent it, actually," Ty mutters. "You said to send it when you ran off, so we did. If they got it, they'll already be preparing."

"Commander, I have to object to all of this," says Doctor Gill. "Emery must get Curosene within"—she checks the display on her city interface—"eleven hours, or the damage to her cells will almost certainly be fatal. If she goes into Ten, there's a high likelihood we won't be able to get her out and return to Base Camp or Blue Haven for the medicine in time. That's not an acceptable risk. She's a child, and not even a member of the SDRT."

"I'm hardly a child," I protest. "And it's not like you're making me do anything. I'm volunteering. I want to go back to The City."

"I have to agree with Doctor Gill," says General Rockshire. "You're not a casualty I'm prepared to accept."

"I don't understand," says Ty. "Don't you have any of those ReqMacs on board that can just make anything you want?"

It's a fair point I hadn't considered.

But Doctor Gill is laughing. "ReqMacs can make simple things like food and clothes, but Curosene is a very complex substance that has to be produced under just the right conditions, similar to DS10. These aren't things you can just whip up whenever you please at a moment's notice."

"It doesn't matter," I say. "The City has Curosene, and I know where to get it."

"They have Curosene?" says Doctor Gill, incredulous.

"Yes, I already got it once—for my brother—and I can get it again."

"There, you see?" says Commander Elben.

"But we still don't have a way through the fire surrounding the Safe Dome," says General Rockshire. "Nothing we've tried has been able to extinguish it. She'll be burned to a crisp before she even gets through the barrier field, and Doctor Gill won't be there to heal her on the other side."

"We could drop her in," my guard says—the first thing he's said since we arrived.

"Yes," I exclaim enthusiastically. "You can drop me in right past the Wall of Fire, exactly where I need to be."

"They'll see you coming. Maybe they'll blast you right out of the sky," says Doctor Gill.

I swallow hard, knowing she's probably right.

"Then we'll return at night," says Commander Elben. "We can create a cover of smoke. They'll think we're just making the same kind of drops we've been doing for days and won't even see her coming."

"And what about the people coming out?" adds Doctor Gill.

"Put a team on the fire problem," Elben directs. "We have a few hours to figure out how to extinguish it. And if we can't, we'll just need to be ready to treat their burns—an easy enough problem to deal with." It's clear that he's set on this plan moving forward.

At least I have one ally here.

"Why are we worried about getting past the fire?" Aiken asks. "Have you all forgotten that this thing can fly? When the barrier field comes down, just land the plane inside. Load up whoever you can, and then take off."

At that, the room erupts into objections.

"Impossible," says Commander Elben, his voice carrying above the rest. "We can't risk getting trapped inside if the barrier field returns to operation faster than anticipated."

The others nod in agreement.

"I'll have the doctors ready," Doctor Gill assures us, though she doesn't look happy about it.

"Must I remind you that this girl is a criminal and should be taken to Base Camp immediately and dealt with?" says General Rockshire in disapproval. Somehow I get the feeling he's trying to protect me rather than wishing to see me punished.

Commander Elben's next words confirm this suspicion. "I think that makes this arrangement perfect. If she successfully completes this mission, it would be fair to pardon her. And if it turns out that DS10 doesn't work as expected and she's unable to clear the barrier field, or she dies in any other way during the mission, I would say justice has been served. She brought it on herself."

"Maxton!" Doctor Gill chides.

"Didn't you hear them?" says Commander Elben, completely unabashed. "The people of Ten are already expecting us. We're not going to disappoint them." And with that, he exits the room, underscoring the finality of his decision.

CHAPTER 10

I eat my dinner in the quiet of the hallway, trying not to consider that, if things go wrong—which they very well could—this sandwich and apple could be my last meal.

"Can I join you?" asks Ty, holding his own dinner tray.

"Of course," I say, patting the hard, cold floor beside me.

We eat in silence for a few minutes, both of us swimming in our own sea of thoughts.

"Are you excited to go back?" asks Ty. He pauses and rubs his temples. "I guess excited isn't the right word."

"Blazing terrified?" I suggest.

He thinks about it for a moment. "Yeah, that sounds about right."

"But I prefer it a million times over compared to sitting around, doing nothing."

"I'm glad I'm not going back," he says.

There are truckloads of reasons why no one would want to return to any Safe Dome, let alone ours, but I get the feeling that Ty has a very specific and personal reason for this sentiment.

"Why's that?"

"I can't face my dad," he says. "Or mom, but Dad's worse because he always had such high hopes for me. And look at me now. I can barely even think straight."

This surprises and saddens me all at once. "Did you know I met your dad?"

"Really?" he asks, surprised.

"Well, not exactly. You see, it was his courier truck that I stowed away in to get across the Wall of Fire. But he didn't know I was there, so it doesn't really count as meeting him, I suppose."

"How do you know it was my dad?"

"I heard him talk to a guard. He mentioned that his son, Ty, was joining the Burning that night. He was anxious to go and see you off. Imagine my surprise when the very first contestant to talk to me was you. But the point is, he sounded so proud of you and talked about what a great guy you are."

"That's what I mean," he laments. "He had so much faith in me, and I let him down. The last thing he saw was me looking like an idiot, trying to sneak into the Smoke. Then he was forced to watch what appeared to be me being executed in disgrace. He must be so ashamed of me now. It's probably best that he thinks I'm dead."

"But none of that was real. The truth is that you saw The City for what it really was long before most people did, and you were willing to put yourself on the line to do something about it. If we do manage to get people out tonight, it'll only be because you were here and knew how to communicate with the Resistance. No matter how tonight turns out, you're a hero, Ty. When your dad learns the truth, he'll be prouder than ever."

"You really think so?"

"Definitely. I've known from the minute I learned the truth about the Council that you were important, and we needed your help. And I was right."

He smiles, leaning his head back against the wall and letting his eyes close. "Thanks, Emery."

I return to eating, finding that the distraction has helped calm my own nerves about tonight as well. No matter what happens, at least I'll always know I did everything I possibly could for the people I love.

"I wish Gar was still here," Ty mutters.

"Huh?"

"He was so much fun to play with," says Ty longingly, reminding me that he's not fully freed of the effects of the Mind Mist just yet.

"I bet you'll see him again soon," I say, which seems to comfort him.

Just then, General Rockshire walks up. "Dark has fallen," he announces somberly. "Are you ready?"

* * *

"Ten seconds," announces Commander Elben over the intercom from behind the closed door to the launch room.

I stand at the open aircraft door, wind whipping

mercilessly through my hair, and watch the orange glow of The City move beneath us as though we're a buzzing insect drawn to the flames. The double rings of fire—one inside the other—gives The City the appearance of a sinister eye watching for our arrival. I shudder at the thought that Ember might already know I'm coming.

I'm clutching a flare which I'm to set off as soon as the transmitter is in place and it's time for Mara to take out the computer. I have Eason's transmitter in my pocket, silver dive bands on all four limbs, and DNA proteins of some other organism in my cells.

I considered asking Doctor Gill which of the organisms that can penetrate the barrier field she used, but I decided it was probably best not to know. I just don't think I could survive the horror if she said I was slowly becoming part dung beetle or rat. So instead, I choose to believe that my cells are full of a plant. Maybe banana DNA will leave me just a little sweeter in the end.

"Seven seconds."

The City seems to fade away as dark clouds spew from the plane with the goal of obscuring the visibility of my descent.

"Five seconds."

My lungs feel like they're shrinking, and I can't get enough oxygen. This drop will send me right into the center of the Flame, very near the Council Building where I hope to find and rescue Eason. Still, I can't help wishing I'd just leapt from the hoverplane earlier, before I had a chance to actually think about what I'm preparing to do.

"Three…"

My head pounds.

"Two…"

My limbs shake.

"One."

I block everything out of my awareness except Eason. I imagine that when I land, he'll be there waiting for me, blissfully happy to see me. And then it's easy…

"Go!"

…to leap from the solid protection of the plane and surrender to the open sky and the forces of gravity.

My stomach clenches and my chest tightens as I begin to fall with no sign of slowing. With the tiniest corner of my mind that isn't completely paralyzed by fear, I wonder if the dive bands I'm wearing are defective. Or if killing me in this dramatic fashion was Commander Elben's twisted plan all along, a punishment for defying him.

But then, much to my relief, I feel a gentle tugging on my wrists and ankles as my momentum gently diminishes. Even though the barrier field is transparent, I can tell exactly where it is because the smoke presses against it and is repelled as though it's a solid wall.

Involuntarily, I tense as I approach the transition point into The City. If Doctor Gill is wrong and I can't pass through, I'll bounce off it and roll down the side of the dome. The dive bands might keep me from breaking open my skull in a crash landing, but that won't protect me from being consumed by the fire.

But I glide effortlessly through the barrier field. It

occurs to me that even if we can't get everyone out right now, or permanently deactivate the Safe Dome, maybe we can get enough DS10 inside to let everyone just walk right out—nothing Ember could do about that. Not unless she's able to correct the insecurity in the barrier field before then.

I glide down to the rooftop of the Burning Center, just about fifty yards off of where I'd hoped to land. But it's close enough. We waited to make the jump until after curfew so the streets would be mostly empty. That also means my cells have been sharing foreign DNA for almost five hours already. According to Doctor Gill, that gives me roughly seven more hours to get Curosene before the transformation becomes fatal. Maybe landing in the Burning Center is a stroke of luck after all. It's best to get my hands on Curosene now before anyone has been alerted to my presence.

"Who's there?" an Enforcer calls from the courtyard below. He must have heard the thud of my feet hitting the rooftop. "It's past curfew for non-essential workers."

I slink as far back into the shadows as possible. My heart pounds, trying to beat its way out of my chest. A part of me wants to call this whole mission off. I'm inside of the Wall of Fire and quite close to the Council Building. I could drop the transmitter, shoot off the flare, use my dive bands to pull me back up to the hoverplane, and let Mara deal with Ember. But that won't free Eason, and when Ember recovers she'll probably make killing Eason her first order of business to set an example. No, I must get to him before I alert the SDRT. It's Eason's only hope.

I have to get out of here before someone comes to investigate. There's a door that must lead to stairs. The only way to reach it is to sprint across the open rooftop. I take a deep breath and then take off, running full out to cross the distance as quickly as possible. But before I reach the door, it swings open. I freeze. With nowhere to hide, I wait, poised to attack if necessary.

A beautiful, sparkling gem steps out into the open. "Em…" she starts to say my name, then lets it trail off.

"Keya!" I say in relief. I have a much higher chance of overpowering my former Burn Master than an Enforcer wielding a blaster. I straighten, but I'm still calculating my chances of escape. I don't have to go through the door. I could leap from the far side of the rooftop with my dive bands to deliver me safely to the ground. But then what?

"How are you?" I ask pleasantly, as though there's nothing out of the ordinary happening here. Maybe I can keep her talking, confuse her, and convince her to let me go.

She comes toward me, her overly-high heels clicking on the concrete as she goes. I tense, prepared to defend myself, but she walks right past me to the edge of the roof and looks down. "It's fine," she calls to the Enforcer below. "Just a cat that knocked over a vent cover."

I stare at her, slack-jawed, not sure what to make of this.

She puts one finger to her lips and motions for me to follow her. Then she strides back toward the door.

Deciding it's probably my best option, I go with her. The last thing I need is for her to change her mind about helping me and call in Terrance Enberg and a whole horde of Enforcers from the Justice Building just next door.

She leads me through the empty hallways, her glimmering gold curls bobbing as she hurries along. Suddenly, she pauses and silently shoves me out of sight to let a maid pass. Then we're off again, heading down a wing of the building I've never been in before. Finally, we reach a door that seems to be her desired destination. She opens it and silently beckons me inside.

I hesitate in the doorway. If I want to escape from her, now would be the time to knock her out and leave her hidden in this room. But then a memory comes back to me of the morning Eason showed me the green house. I'd suspected maybe he and Keya had shared a relationship beyond fellow Burn Masters. He'd denied the accusation, but then he made a point of saying that Keya is "one of the good guys." He followed up the statement by telling me to make sure I remembered that fact if it ever mattered. So I decide to trust Keya because I trust Eason, and I follow her into the dark room where she waits.

She shuts the door behind me, and instead of turning on a light, I hear her clicking heels cross the room away from me. Then there's a sound like she's rustling around in a drawer for something.

"Keya, I…"

"Shh, not yet," she whispers back, the sound barely audible.

Anxiously, I wait, desperately debating what to do. The wrong move here could ruin everything. It's still not too late for me to run.

Then there's the sound of a click that's oddly familiar, even though I can't place it.

"There," she says, no longer whispering, and turns on the overhead light.

It's then that I see what she's holding and recognize the sound. Her deactivated intercuff is in one hand, and a tarnished, bronze intercuff key—Eason's intercuff key—is in the other. Seeing that makes me certain I was right to trust her. Eason must have given it to her before the Refinement, much the way he gave me his wooden box with the transmitter, knowing things might not go as he'd planned—which they didn't.

We're in a room that looks very much like the bedroom I stayed in during my time as a Burning contestant, except this room is filled with little figurines and pretty sparkling gems, and other beautiful and pointless objects adorning every surface. This must be Keya's bedroom.

She tosses the deactivated intercuff on her bed and pockets Eason's key as she rushes back over to me. "Emery!" she exclaims. "What are you doing here? And what are you wearing? And your hair…" She shakes her head, trying to stay focused on the issue at hand.

"I had help from the Architect," I say, knowing that will mean more to her than trying to explain all about the SDRT.

"What?" she says in surprise.

"Keya, what's happened in The City since Ember revealed herself?"

She inhales a deep breath. "It's been chaos," she says. "She began by giving everyone in The City an option."

That surprises me, and I wonder what choice she might have offered.

"She said that anyone who wanted her protection should come to the Flame, and anyone who wanted to leave The City should go to the Smoke. For a few hours, all the gateways in the Wall of Fire were open to anyone to come and go as they pleased. But whichever side you chose, that's where you had to stay."

"And you chose to stay here?" I ask, wondering if my trust in her was mistaken. Who would choose the tyranny of Ember over freedom?

"Not because I love The City or trust that computer. It's because I don't trust it, and I knew it was only from here that I'd have any real hope of doing something about the situation."

I suppose that makes sense. "So what has happened to everyone in the Smoke?" I ask. "I know she hasn't set them free."

"I don't think she ever planned to. She just wanted everyone to reveal how they really felt. Now, she's going to make an example of them. The gateways between the

Smoke and Flame have been sealed. No supplies are being sent to the Smoke. I don't know for sure, but I'm guessing it must be anarchy over there. The City's recycling programs have ground to a complete stand-still. The two parts of The City aren't meant to survive without each other. We can't go on like this for long," she says with a look of concern.

"Ember's not going to let it go on long," I say. "Earlier today, we intercepted a message she sent to the Smoke. She said that if everyone doesn't return to their work by tomorrow morning, she's going to start killing people, beginning with Eason." A lump forms in my throat. I cough to clear it, but it won't budge.

Keya gasps and covers her mouth.

"What about food?" I ask. "Is everyone still being given meal rations?"

She nods with a look of distaste.

"Are people still getting sick?"

"Yes, a few. One died. Ember said it's something the Resistance did to the food in order to destroy The City."

"It wasn't the Resistance; it was the computer," I say, but my conviction wavers as I say it. If I'm being honest, I don't really know anything about the Resistance—who they are, or what they would or wouldn't do. Even Ty admitted he doesn't know who's in charge. Would they resort to poisoning people in order to turn the citizens against the leaders—first the Council, and then Ember? I can't entirely rule it out.

Except, why would Ember instruct the same food to

be brought to the Flame and served here?

I glance at the bed where Keya's intercuff sits. It won't be long before the Enforcers realize she isn't wearing it and come looking.

"Keya, I need your help," I say, grabbing her shoulders and shaking. "We think we have a way to shut down the computer, but only for a little while. We have to be prepared to get as many people out as possible while the barrier field is down."

"But how can we do that? Will the Wall of Fire be down, too?"

"I don't know," I admit. "I don't think we can count on that. You can use the tunnels."

"Tunnels? There aren't—"

"Yes, there are. There's one in the basement of this building that leads directly to the school in the Smoke." I tell her how to locate the plank in the wall that she'll need to remove in order to access it. "Gather whoever you can trust and get out of here."

"And what about you?"

"I'll get out," I assure her. I'm not foolish enough to think I'll have time to make it all the way to the outer edge of The City. That's why I'm counting on my dive bands to take me safely out of reach. I just hope they can handle Eason and my weight combined. But I don't waste time explaining all of this to Keya now. "Right now, I have to find Eason."

"He'll be in the Council Building."

"That's what I figured. What's the best way to get in?"

"There's no way for you to get in," she mutters, deep in thought. "Unless…" She races back over to the bed and picks up her intercuff. "You can wear this. I have top-level access to everywhere in the Flame. This will get you where you need to go."

I hate the idea of being shackled with an intercuff again, but I know she's right, and she's taking an enormous risk for me and Eason. If I'm caught—or she's caught without her band—she'll wish the worst thing Ember could do is send her to the Ash.

She moves to put it on me.

"Hold on." I pull my wrist away. Once she puts it on, nothing we say will be private anymore. "I need one more thing first. Where is Doctor Hollen?"

"He's gone."

"Where?"

"He chose to go to the Smoke. He said he wanted to be with his son again."

I wonder if she knows that Doctor Hollen has two sons, and she's met them both. But now isn't the time for that discussion. I'm glad Van is with his family in the Smoke. But that still leaves me with a very big problem right now. "Who's running the Medical Center here?" I ask.

"No one."

"What?"

"It'll be months before another round of the Burning begins—if that's even still a thing now. Who knows?" She shrugs. "But in the meantime, while we're just training the newly assigned Burn Master and other workers, the Medical Center here is empty. We just use the main Medical Center like everyone else in the Flame."

"I need some medicine," I say. "If it's empty, I should be able to sneak in and grab what I need. I know where Doctor Hollen kept it."

She shakes her head. "When it's closed, no supplies are kept there. Unless you just need an empty bed and some space to yourself, you won't find it here."

"Blazes," I mutter. There's no way I can get all the way across the Flame to the Medical Center unseen. Maybe Keya could go and bring it back, but what could she tell them that would convince them to hand over Curosene? Especially if people are sick like Whyle was, and that's all that can help them, it'll be guarded carefully.

I'll just have to go on without it. With any degree of luck, Eason and I will be out of here with plenty of time remaining to travel to Base Camp before my cells become too damaged.

I hold out my wrist. "Okay, time to go."

CHAPTER 11

Without a word—now that Keya's intercuff is attached to my wrist and Eason's key tucked in my pocket—she drapes a shimmering green robe over my clothes and twists my hair up into a fancy little bun in hopes of helping me blend in better as I travel the three blocks to the Council Building. Then she walks me to the exit.

I embrace her, grateful for her help.

"Good luck," she mouths soundlessly, and pushes me toward the door that exits the building into a walkway only Burning Center staff has access to.

I hold up my wrist to the panel next to the door. The panel and the intercuff flash green, and the door swings open. Forcing a confident posture, I stride out into the open. A long sidewalk runs between the Burning Center and the Justice Building. It's through here that they can come and go each day without having to contend with the Enforcers and razor-wire fences that keep the contestants secure. At the far end, this alleyway opens up into the main streets of the Flame. From there it's just a few blocks to the Council Building.

I'm almost to the street when a door to the Justice

Building opens, and a woman wearing the red and gold of an Enforcer's uniform steps out. I pause and hold my breath, as though that might make me less visible. In the single second that passes before she sees me, my features try on a dozen expressions, searching for something that feels natural and nonthreatening. When she turns to look at me, I'm smiling the kind of smile I used to give others in the food lines at the Nutrition Station—pleasant, but unapproachable.

She gives a brief nod and exits the alley without another glance in my direction.

Alone, I gasp and clutch my chest to slow my racing heart. I have to hold it together. In ten more steps I'll be out in the open. Though it's late, I can see that curfew isn't very strictly enforced here, and there are still people moving about. If I have a panic attack every time one of them lays eyes on me, I'll be caught in no time. I have to look like I belong, like I haven't a care in the world.

I think of Commander Elben and step forward in my best imitation of his overly-confident stride. Torches glow at every corner, illuminating the streets. I pass a mother and her two children, a pair of teenagers walking hand-in-hand, and two Enforcers encouraging everyone to head home. None of them pay me any special attention.

When the Council Building comes into view, it's all I can do not to break into a run. Eason is so close. It's as though I can feel his presence drawing me in like a magnet I'm powerless to resist. But I force my feet to move at a steady, measured pace.

Wisps of black smoke still swirl in the sky above, outlining the shape of the Safe Dome. Only a few glistening stars manage to peek through. I can't see the plane, but I know it's up there. They must be getting anxious waiting for the signal. I'll need to send it soon, one way or the other.

At the door, I hold my wrist up to the panel, bracing myself for whatever I might face on the other side. But the panel turns red, denying me entrance. I rip my wrist away for a moment and then bring it back to try again, but the door still won't open. Either Keya's access level isn't what she thought, or someone knows I'm here. Either way, I've got to find another way in, and fast. I race around to the back of the building where my presence is shrouded in shadows. There's another door. I try it, but to no avail.

I find a rock in a decorative planter box nearby and lob it at the nearest window. Though my aim is perfect and my pitch strong, the rock bounces back to me, repelled by a barrier field. I retrieve it and try again, this time aiming for a second-story window. And this time, the glass shatters. Now it's just a matter of getting up there.

"What was that?" someone yells, and footsteps begin moving swiftly in my direction.

I take hold of a drainpipe and begin scurrying up. By the time the Enforcer reaches the place where I stood, I'm twelve feet above, crouched on the ledge of the building's second floor. He looks around in confusion. There are no lingering signs of my presence, and since the window broke inward, there's no broken glass on the street below to alert him.

My arms begin to ache, and my fingers, gripping the rough brick wall, start to lose purchase. I'm going to have to move if I don't want to fall, but he's not leaving. I've got to find some way to draw his attention away from here. Slowly, carefully, I manage to pull from my pocket the one and only thing I have in my possession that isn't entirely necessary for my immediate survival. Even though it pains me to do it, I toss the crumpled mass of Eason's note as far as I can. Thankfully it hits a recycle bin with a soft thud, pulling the Enforcer's attention all the way across the street. Dutifully, he takes off running to check it out.

The instant he's turned his back and started moving away, I scamper along the ledge to the broken window. It's only partially broken. I doubt even little Quinn could fit through without getting cut. But at least I know there's no barrier field here. I pull up the robe Keya gave me so it covers my face. Then, thinking of nothing but reaching Eason as quickly as possible, I grit my teeth and throw myself, shoulder first, into the window. It gives way, and I tumble to the ground where shards of broken glass await me, slicing into me in a dozen places.

I glance around to make sure I'm alone. Then I get to my feet and pull the glass from my flesh. None of the cuts are too deep, and Doctor Gill will fix them right up as soon as I get out of here. It's then that I see the silver dive bands on my wrists and ankles and realize that I probably could have reversed them and used them to float up to the window. If nothing else, they would have prevented me from getting hurt if I'd fallen, but wouldn't have protected me from the Enforcer's blaster if he'd seen me. Regardless, I have to remember that I'm wearing them and to use them when it counts.

The room is dimly lit, but I appear to be in someone's office. In fact, the nameplate on the desk reads: Traeger Sterling. I walk over to it, curiosity compelling me to see what occupied his desk the day he was discarded by Ember. There are piles of papers all covered in a thick layer of dust, as though no one has used or disturbed this room in years.

I pick up the top paper and blow the dust from it, fighting to not cough as the fine particles swirl in the air around me. It's a handwritten letter addressed to Bretton Crandell. The date at the top is nearly two years ago.

Why would Traeger be writing to Bretton so long after he'd been sent to the Ash?

I skim the lines, and several words seem to draw my eyes to them like magnets: Ember, Architect, and Eason.

"Over here!" someone yells in the street below. "The sound came from up there."

I don't have to look out to know people are congregating below the broken window, and soon, the building will be swarming with Enforcers. I shove the letter in my pocket without reading it.

I'd hoped to find Eason before I lit the flare, but if I'm caught—which is a likely scenario, if I'm being honest—I may not be able to get to a window or door to signal Mara, and the transmitter might be taken or destroyed. As much as I care about Eason, I have to think of everyone else as well. I take the transmitter out of my pocket and bury it in one of Traeger's desk drawers. Then I run to the window, pull the two ends of the flare apart, and watch a green spark soar into the air and crash against the barrier field above. Wherever the plane is, it must have seen that. Everyone in The City probably saw it. And that means I have thirty minutes to find Eason and get out. At least I won't have to contend with Ember along the way, but that doesn't mean it's going to be easy.

I run to the door and am relieved to find it's not locked from this side. I throw it open and bound out into the empty, dark hallway. My footsteps echo in the stillness. I keep glancing over my shoulder, but no one comes. In fact, the only sounds I hear seem to be coming from outside.

The hallway is lined with doors, and I try each one as I pass, but none of them will open for me. Frustrated, I keep moving, realizing I could have already passed Eason and I'd never know it.

I reach the stairwell and leap down several steps at a time. On the ground floor, there's another long, empty hallway. Again, every door is locked. Occasionally I think I hear the sound of banging or screaming, but it's always so faint I can't be sure it isn't just in my harried imagination.

"Eason!" I yell; no point in staying quiet now that they

already know I'm here.

Time seems to slow, the seconds passing like hours. I wonder exactly how it was that I convinced myself I could save Eason if I could just return to The City.

And I wonder why no one has come for me yet. In fact, even the noise of Enforcers gathering below the broken window outside has faded away. Maybe it means there's nothing here. Really, there's no reason that Ember's computer system or her captives have to be in this building in particular. Traeger's office hasn't been used in ages. Maybe they abandoned this place in favor of somewhere secret where no one would think to look for them.

Just when I'm about to give up in despair, I hold Keya's intercuff to the panel next to the very last door, and it clicks open. My heart leaps and I'm suddenly terrified, but I don't let that stop me from pushing my way inside.

"Ah. Not Keya after all," says a woman's icy voice.

CHAPTER 12

Ember looks just as she did when I last saw the giant image of her head projected into the night sky—delicate white skin, deep red lips, and features so sharp they could cut stone. But now she's sitting on a white satin sofa next to a brightly glowing fireplace and gazing at me with her cold, inhuman eyes. She must have built herself a robot body. She stands and walks toward me. Her movements are so lifelike that I probably wouldn't give her a second glance if I saw her walking down the street.

Upon seeing her, all my fear is supplanted by an electrifying rage so intense I can feel nothing else, but I'm careful not to betray my emotions. Surely she could use anything I feel to manipulate me.

Mara said she could shut down the computer for half an hour. It can't have been more than ten minutes since I lit the flare. That means either Mara hasn't stunned her yet and it'll happen any second, or she tried and failed. Either way I need to find Eason, and she's the only one who knows where he is.

"Hi, Ember," I say. "I have to say, I'm a little surprised to see you. You look different when you're not a giant floating head in the sky."

"Yes, this form is much better for dealing directly with humans."

"What do you want?" I ask.

"The same thing I've always wanted," she says. "To protect people. Yet you all constantly make it so difficult. Even when I give people exactly what they want, they still insist on endangering themselves and others. Take you, for example. I thought you wanted to be out of the Safe Dome. All your actions suggested that. So I gave you exactly what you wanted, even though it broke my heart to do it."

A disbelieving laugh escapes my lips. "You don't have a heart. You're a computer—a machine. You can never understand what it means to be human."

She tilts her head to the side and purses her lips, as though she's truly considering my words. "Maybe that's true. But do *you* really know what it means to be human? As far as I can tell, you don't behave like most humans. Under the conditions I have constructed, you never should have had the will to keep fighting the way that you have. Most people give up, but you don't. You are an outlier—an oddity. Why do you insist on being so difficult? I gave you everything—food, shelter, protection…"

"Until you started killing us," I accuse. "If you claim to be protecting us, then why are you poisoning the food?" I lash out before I've thought it through.

"It's only dangerous to people who are dangerous," she

says, as though my accusation confuses her.

I want to say more, to ask more. To find out exactly why she felt it necessary to try to kill the kindest and most loving eight-year-old on the planet. How could Whyle be dangerous to anyone? But I fight the impulse to appease my curiosity, because understanding why makes no difference now.

Any second, Ember will deactivate and the barrier field will disappear, and if I don't have Eason out of here before they return, I can guess exactly how necessary she'll find killing both Eason and me.

"I've noticed you have a little problem with the Smoke," I say. "I could help you. They know me; they trust me; they'll listen to me."

She laughs. "No one here trusts anyone; I've seen to that. But let's just pretend for a minute that you're right. Why do you want to help me?"

"I don't want anyone else to get hurt. I care about people, too."

"Really? You care about all the people out there?" She makes a sweeping gesture toward the window. "I know the name of every person in The City. I care for them all."

"I care, too," I insist, though I certainly don't know even close to every name.

"Really?" she says, her voice colder than usual, if that's even possible. "So you're telling me that you're capable of weighing the good of everyone above your own personal, selfish preferences? Because I think you don't care about any of them. I think you came here for a single person."

She raises one hand, and the door behind me swings open.

Startled, I jump and turn to see Eason—bound and gagged, his face colored in varying shades of purples, greens, and yellows from bruises, old and new—being escorted in by Terrance Enberg.

Eason's in the room with me, so close I could reach out and touch him. This is the perfect moment for Mara to stun Ember. Why hasn't she done it already? Didn't they see the flare? Or has something else gone wrong?

For only the briefest second, Eason and I lock eyes. I want to run to him, to tear apart his bindings and cling to him. But in front of Ember, I don't dare give the slightest indication that I'm moved at all by this sight.

"Emery?" mutters Terrance, and there's no mistaking the surprise and twisted satisfaction in his expression. I'm sure he never expected to see me again, and he's anticipating administering the most severe punishment imaginable.

"Thank you, Terrance," says Ember. "You may go."

His mouth turns down into a disappointed frown, but he doesn't argue.

"Now tell me, Emery," she says, slowly stepping closer. "How did you get back inside the barrier field?"

So she doesn't know. And if she doesn't know then she can't adapt the barrier field, and the SDRT hasn't lost this advantage. We can do it again and again, as many times as it takes to end this.

I stare back silently, willing Mara to rescue us.

I can feel the slight weight of Eason's intercuff key in my pocket, and my fingers itch to reach for it and remove my intercuff before Ember begins using it to force an answer from my lips. But I can't do that where she can see.

"Not feeling talkative," she observes. "How about now?"

I brace myself for the jolt of pain through every nerve in my body, but it doesn't come. Instead, Eason cries out and crumples to his knees. It's his intercuff I need to remove.

"No!" I scream, and run to him, pulling the gag from his mouth.

"It's okay," he whispers breathlessly. "I'm okay. Don't say anything."

But despite his assurances, I'm not comforted. That was only the lowest setting of the intercuff. Maybe I can slip him the key and stand to block her view while he removes it. But she steps closer and kneels at his side, removing any such opportunity. I'll have to find another way to distract her.

"You see, I care about everyone equally," Ember says. "And that means if I have to sacrifice one to get the information I need to protect thousands, I won't hesitate. Isn't that right, Eason?" She runs the backs of her fingers down Eason's cheek in an eerie caress, turning my stomach. "Wouldn't it have saved you a lot of pain if you had just told me about that little transmitter to begin with? But in the end, you did talk. They always do." She turns her empty gaze on me and waits, expectant.

I stare back, jaw clenched, saying nothing.

"How about this," she says, and raises both arms. Suddenly, the sofa disappears and is replaced with all sorts of malevolent devices covered in straps, spikes, and blades. She crosses the room. "This is an interesting device that slowly pulls a person's arms and legs free of their sockets until it has ripped the limbs clean off the body. Then you bleed to death, if your internal organs haven't already ruptured. Maybe watching Eason endure this will loosen your tongue, and you'll tell me how you got through the fire and the barrier field."

She hasn't even tried to harm me once, though I'm still wearing an intercuff. I hate how easily she understood that the most torturous thing she could do to me would be to force me to watch Eason suffer.

"Don't say anything," Eason whimpers.

"Eason," Ember says as though rebuking a child, "I'm beginning to think you actually like pain, because you do so many things to bring it on yourself."

He screams again, this time longer, leaving his breathing labored afterwards.

I hold him to me and slowly slip the intercuff key from my pocket. I take his hand and pass it to him. His expression is confused when the thin metal pin rests in his palm, but only for an instant.

I turn my back on him, hoping to keep Ember's gaze off him long enough for him to free himself. "If you want to know how I did it, I'll tell you, but I have some questions first," I say, in an effort to distract her.

She laughs. "This is what I can't understand about humans," she says, sounding oddly tired. "They do so many things that aren't in their best interest. Take you, Emery. You seem to be a good example of everything stupid and wrong with humans. I'm not sure how you got here, but maybe an equally important question is why. You were free, and yet you came back even though there is a"—she suddenly freezes as still as a statue, and I wonder if Mara has done it, but then she moves again and continues speaking—"zero point zero one percent chance you will leave here alive tonight."

Her words are chilling, but I'm actually a little surprised she calculates my odds to be that high, considering she knows nothing about the robot we have on our side and the foreign DNA in my cells, or Eason's intercuff key. It also explains why she excused Terrance and doesn't see a need for a single Enforcer around her. She is utterly confident in her ability to subdue and destroy us herself. But if Mara doesn't come through soon, she might be right.

Ember smiles. "Let's get started."

She reaches down and picks up Eason as though he weighs no more than a toddler and carries him to the torture device she just described in such gruesome detail. His intercuff and the key remain on the ground behind him, and Ember doesn't seem to notice. Quickly, I kick the intercuff out of sight and scoop up the key, returning it to my pocket.

Eason struggles ineffectually against her grip. Single-handedly and with seemingly no effort at all, she secures both his ankles with straps that connect to the table. It doesn't matter that his intercuff is gone; Ember will have no trouble restraining and torturing him without it.

Mara, come on, I silently plead.

She moves on to Eason's hands, removing one set of bindings in preparation for securing him in a new, more terrifying way.

I can't count on Mara to save us. I can't count on anyone else. Ember calculated my odds of escaping here as one one-thousandth of a percent. And if that's all I've got, then I'd better not waste any of it frozen in shock. I charge her from behind, hoping to knock her over, to buy us a few more seconds, at least. She continues working on securing his wrists, and simultaneously kicks out her leg to connect with my gut, bending her leg at an angle that would be impossible for a human. But instead of hitting her—or her hitting me—I pass completely through her.

CHAPTER 13

She drops Eason's insecurely bound hands and turns to me in shock. "What did you do?" she demands.

It takes me a minute to understand. This form of Ember isn't real. It's not a robot. She is nothing more than projections on a carefully constructed set of barrier fields, just like the changing maze or all the obstacles of the Gold Trial. And she can't touch me now.

She swings her arms wildly toward me, but I feel nothing except the slightest tickle as they pass right through me, as though one of us is a ghost.

Ignoring her attack, I turn to Eason, who has wasted no time wriggling his hands free. He sits up and frees his legs from the straps that bind them. "Take my hand," I say, remembering how Ty's connection to me pulled him through the barrier field when we were expelled from The City. Even though he hadn't had the antidote, with our hands clasped the barrier couldn't make a clear distinction between where I ended and he began.

Without hesitation, he leaps from the sinister table and grabs my outstretched hand with much more strength than I would have expected him capable of just seconds ago. I wonder if his frail appearance was partially an act.

An evil-looking device with spikes covering the surface flies toward us. It appears Ember can control the objects in this room with a mere thought.

We leap to the side, but we're too late. The weapon hits me directly, though "hit" isn't the right word, because it sails right through me as though I'm nothing but air. After it's passed through me, it does the same to Eason.

He flinches, and then exhales in relief when he finds that, much to his astonishment, he's completely unharmed.

I'm expecting more attacks, but they don't come. Instead, Ember freezes just as she did when she was calculating my odds of escape, but this time for much longer. I suppose calculating how Eason and I are now completely unaffected by any barrier field is more than her circuits can handle.

I slip Eason's intercuff key from my pocket and remove my intercuff before Ember recovers enough to realize she could still control me with this.

"We have to go!" Eason says, and pulls me toward the door.

I pull him back. "Terrance might still be there, waiting." Barrier fields may not be able to affect us, but blasters certainly can. "The window," I whisper.

We race toward it past Ember, who's still standing like a ghostly statue. The window is made of a solid pane of glass with no way to open it. There's a spiked hammer on the ground next to me, and I reach for it, but find that

I'm just as unable to grasp it as Ember is to touch me.

"I'm going to let go for a second," I say, keeping my voice low. "When I do, throw that hammer at the window to break it, then grab my hand again."

He nods.

Reluctantly, I unclasp his hand. He spins to the side, grabs the hammer, and lobs it across the room, sending it crashing into the glass and shattering it to pieces. But rather than soaring through to the outside, the hammer connects with the barrier field that I learned earlier surrounds the bottom floor of this building and bounces back with full momentum. It soars straight through me and connects with the paralyzed form of Ember, jogging her from her trance.

I lunge to reach for Eason, but I'm not as fast as she is, and before I have him she's already taken hold of him, grasping him around the middle in a viselike grip.

He cries out and struggles against her, but she's so much stronger than he is—stronger than any human can be. Just as I hear the sickening sound of cracking bones, I take him by both hands and pull as hard as I can, but she holds him fast. Still maintaining my grip on him, I kick my foot right through her chest. As soon as I connect with her, she loses her ability to hold Eason. Somehow, this is what it took to solidify our connection and confuse the barrier fields.

Free of her crushing hold, I pull Eason toward the window. I leap through, but Eason is struggling to move or breathe, and I have to slow down and help pull him through. Behind him, Ember is trying in vain to attack. The streets behind me are filled with shouts and the sound of heavy footsteps. No doubt Ember has called in her army of Enforcers, and we will not be able to escape them.

The instant Eason and I are out of the Council Building, I flip my dive bands—gold side out—and wrap my arms around Eason. "Hold on tight," I warn.

"What?" he exclaims in surprise as we begin to ascend.

"We're getting out of here," I assure him.

I'm expecting the bands to take us all the way up to the hoverplane, but instead they deposit us on the roof of the Council Building. I look around in surprise. The sky is clear of the dark smoke now, and there's no hoverplane in sight. The dive bands will only take us as high as there's a place for us to land. At the moment, that's the rooftop. The plane must have landed so they can be ready to help the people fleeing The City. Maybe they've found a way to extinguish the fire, and that accounts for the delay. But does that also mean that they didn't see the flare when I lit it?

I can't worry about any of that now. There's nothing I can do about it, and our situation requires all my focus if I'm going to keep the two of us alive.

"Can you run?" I ask Eason.

He nods without hesitation, but there's no disguising the glistening of his eyes or the way he's clenching his jaw. He's in serious pain. But if we don't get moving, we'll both be dead. I keep an arm around him to help him along as we run across the rooftop. We reach the edge, and I can see the street below filling with Enforcers. They're marching the streets, but I'm pretty sure they haven't figured out where we are yet because they aren't looking up.

I survey the area for any way down that doesn't put us directly in the hands of the Enforcers, but there's none.

"Eason, we're going to jump," I tell him.

"Jump?" he says in alarm.

"Trust me," I say, even though I'm making this up as I go.

Apparently he does, because he doesn't fight me. With the dive bands still on, gold side out for ascent, we run toward the building's edge and leap out as far as we can toward the next rooftop. My breath catches as we start to descend toward the ground below, but then we rise again and are deposited on the next rooftop, just as I'd hoped we would be.

We didn't drift low enough for The Enforcers to get their hands on us, but they know where we are now. The low whine of several blaster shots slice through the night—kill shots.

"No!" Terrance yells. "Ember wants them alive. Stun only!"

Interesting. So apparently Ember considers us valuable. Not that it makes me anymore desirous to stick around.

Eason is gasping for air and pressing and holding his chest.

"It's just a little farther to the Wall of Fire," I say. "We have to keep moving."

He nods and forces himself to stand straighter.

I lead us from rooftop to rooftop back toward the Burning Center, which is the building nearest the Wall of Fire—the only destination meant for people from the Smoke. In the streets below, Enforcers scurry like ants racing around to keep up with us. It's not until we land on the flat concrete top of the Burning Center that they finally managed to get ahead of us, and an Enforcer waits for us, blaster in hand.

I freeze and hold Eason tighter. He sways from the fatigue and pain and leans heavily on me. The Enforcer stands between us and the roof's edge. If we could only reach it, we could jump far enough to sail right through the lapping, projected flames of the Wall of Fire, where the Enforcers couldn't follow us. At best Ember could open the nearest gateway, but by the time they made it through and circled back around, we'd be long gone and well hidden. But we'll never make it without being blasted. We can't even make it to the door that leads down into the building. And even if we could, we ditched our intercuffs and can't open it.

"Stop there! You can't escape," the Enforcer yells.

Uncontrollably, I break into hysterical laughter, not because he's wrong, but because I recognize his voice. This is the very same Enforcer who apprehended me at the Medical Center the night I crossed the Wall of Fire, and who escorted me to the Ash. It seems we're destined to keep meeting like this. My laughter, psychotic as it may be, seems to unnerve him, and he looks around as though he's missing something.

It's in that moment of distraction that the door to the rooftop opens. A girl emerges, carrying a bucket and mop. I recognize her instantly.

"Petra!" I yell.

"Emery?" she whispers in surprise.

"Step aside," the Enforcer calls.

She jumps and turns to see a blaster pointed straight at her chest. She glances over her shoulder at me for the briefest moment, and then does something I never in my life would have expected. The Enforcer doesn't expect it either, so when Petra suddenly whirls with the long, solid handle of the mop stretched out, it connects hard with the side of his head and knocks him to the ground.

She stares down at his unconscious body. The mop she's holding falls from her grasp and clatters on the ground. Then she gasps and brings her hands up to cover her mouth, eyes widening as she realizes what she's just done.

I can hear footsteps climbing the stairs.

"Let's go!" I yell. Eason has recovered enough to hobble along on his own again. I keep hold around his waist and grab onto Petra as we run past her.

"What are you doing?" she asks, her voice shaking as we near the edge of the building.

"Trust me, and…jump!" I yell.

She does. We soar forward, and with no nearby

rooftop to be raised up to, we're lowered to the ground. My dive bands struggle under the weight of all three of us, and we descend faster than before, hitting the ground a few feet short of the Wall of Fire.

More Enforcers than I can count race toward us, closing in from three sides. The perfect night air is filled with the high-pitched shrill of stun shots.

"We're almost there," I call, regaining my footing and pressing forward to the safety that lies beyond the orange glow before us.

And just as I'm about to touch the tingling, projected flames, another blaster shot pierces the air, and everything disappears.

CHAPTER 14

Awareness comes back to me in layers. First, I feel a touch on my face, gentle and caressing. Then I hear Eason's breath on my ear as he whispers my name. Next, I open my eyes to see his perfect—though bruised—face smiling down at me. And finally, I realize that if he's this calm, we must have made it across the Wall of Fire. We must be somewhere safe.

I sit up so fast that my head starts spinning, but I don't care. I throw myself at Eason, drawing him into an enormous embrace and kissing any part of him I can reach—his hair, his cheeks, his lips.

But all too soon he pushes me away, grimacing.

I feel the edges of my heart fissure as the rejection sets in. I pull away, embarrassed. "I'm sorry. I should have... I shouldn't have..."

"Emery," he whispers.

I can't look at him. "I—"

"Emery," he says again, placing his palm gently against my cheek and turning my face to his. When I finally do look into his eyes, they're warm and inviting. "I'm just a little wounded right now, that's all. You'll have to be gentle for a while."

"Oh," I mutter, and my head begins to clear. I gasp. "Oh, blazes, I can't believe I forgot. I'm so sorry! I was just so happy to see you. Are you okay? Can I do anything for you?"

He pulls me to him, carefully wrapping an arm around me. "This is perfect," he whispers in contentment, and I let myself relax into him and everything in the world feels so right.

But the moment can't last, because everything is not right. So many things are wrong. And I don't have much time left. We'll have to postpone the rest of our reunion.

I get to my feet and look around, but there's not much to see—makeshift brick and wood walls, dirt floor, and two lanterns for light.

"Where are we?" I ask in confusion.

"This is the Resistance headquarters," he says.

"What? How did you find it? How did you know to bring me here?"

"I told him," comes a woman's voice.

I start at the unexpected sound and turn. It takes me a minute in the dim lighting to realize why this woman looks so familiar. "Gina?" I ask.

"Hi, Emery," replies Gina Crandell—Eason's mother.

"What are you doing here?"

"Well, there's no point in keeping this secret anymore," she says. "I'm the leader of the Resistance."

With all Gina knew about the Council, and all Bretton and Eason have sacrificed to free The City, it shouldn't surprise me that Gina would be the leader of the

Resistance. It shouldn't, but it does. And yet I suddenly understand why Ember saw Eason as an important pawn to use against the rebels. She must have figured out that their leader was his mother, and hoped to twist her love for him to subdue the rebellion.

Gina comes to my side and wraps me in a hug. "Thank you so much for saving my son," she says, her voice heavily laden with emotion. I don't point out that I had my own motives that had nothing to do with her. I doubt it'll make any difference to her why I saved Eason, just so long as he's safe now.

"Where is this place, exactly?" I ask. It has a familiar feel, even though I can't quite say why.

"Missed me, eh?" comes another voice, and a figure I would recognize anywhere steps from behind a partition, hunched, hobbling on one leg, and gaunt-faced.

"Kenna!" The exclamation comes out like a high-pitched squeal. I go to her and wrap her in a hug. This must be the inside of her house that, from the outside, looks like nothing more than a pile of rubble. A perfect place for the Resistance to hide.

"All right. All right, girlie. That's enough," she says, waving her cane around wildly in the air.

"It's so good to see you."

"You didn't happen to bring any more fat rats with you?" she asks, licking her lips.

My stomach threatens to convulse. I've had the misfortune of eating rats, and while I did it out of necessity, I can't imagine ever looking forward to it with the longing in her eyes.

"No, sorry," I mutter. Then I turn back to Gina. "You should all be at the edge of The City," I say in a rush. "Didn't you get our transmission? It was in Resistance code. The barrier field should be coming down at any moment, but it won't be down long, so we need to get as many people out as possible when we have the chance." I just hope we haven't missed our window of opportunity while I was stunned and unconscious.

No one moves.

"Let's go!" I cry, and start pulling Eason toward the door. "Where's Petra?" I ask, looking for her and not finding her anywhere.

"After she helped get you and Eason here, I sent her with a group that's heading for the edge," says Gina. "We did get your message, and we're moving as many people as we can. I stayed here to direct the effort."

"What about my family?" I ask, feeling a pang of guilt that it's taken me this long to think of them. "How do I get out of here? I need to go find them. How many Enforcers are out?"

Gina places a comforting hand on my shoulder, stopping me. "We've already collected your family. And there aren't any Enforcers in the Smoke. Not since Ember sealed off the gateways through the Wall of Fire."

"Okay, then we need to get going to the outer edge," I say. "I'm surprised the barrier hasn't come down yet, but we might as well try to make it if we can."

"There's a truck on its way for us," she says. "We had a

report that the hoverplane landed on the south side of The City, so that's where we'll head."

*   *   *

We huddle in the stuffy back of the truck, bumping along over the cracked streets. Every available inch of space is occupied. I'm nestled next to Eason, careful not to put too much pressure anywhere that might hurt him. Gina managed to find a pain pill for him, but I can tell by the shallowness of his breathing that it hasn't fully relieved his suffering.

Gina tells me that the Resistance has three trucks in their possession, and they've been driving virtually non-stop since Ty's message came. As we travel, I fill them in on everything that's happened since I left The City, and I get a few questions of my own answered. It turns out that Ember faced a very upsetting surprise when she discovered that, not only had everyone from the Ash been treated with the inoculation Ollie and Roe developed against any mind-controlling agents, but that the Resistance has been slowly giving people in the Smoke the antidote for months.

"So you developed the antidote?" I ask Gina.

"Not me personally, but the Resistance, yes," she confirms.

"But how did you know about the Mind Mist?"

"It wasn't easy," she says. "I've been working for years to unravel the many secrets of The City and discover its weaknesses. It's taken our entire network, including some anonymous tips from people in the Flame. First, we discovered that most of our food comes through the gateway, so it had to be coming from the Ash, but I needed to know why and how. We came up with a plan to have some of our people sent to the Ash on purpose. They committed various offenses against The City, or failed the Burning if they happened to be seventeen years old and able to join. Once there, they transmitted back coded messages, and that's how we learned about the farm."

"Transmitted?" I ask in surprise.

"Yes, Eason's not the only one who had access to the plans for how to build transmitters," she points out. "The strangest thing was that we only ever received messages on the first day they arrived in the Ash. After that, we could never reach them again. We would send more people, and they confirmed that the others were still there, but it was as though they'd forgotten—not about the Resistance, per se, but that they actually cared. And then the next day, we'd lose contact again."

"The Mind Mist comes at night, so that makes sense," I observe.

"Finally, we got our hands on some of the food fresh from the Ash," she goes on. "Our researchers found that it was covered in a fine layer of a mind-controlling agent. It was only on the outside, not the inside, so they concluded it must have been in the air rather than something done to the food as it was being grown. From there, it took a few more months to develop the antidote."

I have lots of questions about who else on the farm were members of the Resistance, and what exactly their plan was to free The City. "So you gave the antidote to Eason so he could complete his mission in the Ash," I say. "But Eason, why didn't you have us take it before the Refinement? It could have saved me a lot of trouble if I'd already had it before I was sent to the Ash."

"That was my fault," says Gina. "I told him to wait until he got there in case they had some way of detecting it on a body scan or when you pass through the gateway. I couldn't risk tipping our hand. It's the same reason we didn't give it to any of our own people—like Ty. Our plan was to get enough people out in the Ash to take over the farm. Then we would send someone with enough antidote for everyone and give it to all of them at once."

"I guess that makes sense," I say.

We fall silent. There's so much information and so many questions swirling around in my head that I can hardly make sense of it all. Based on Eason and Gina's expressions, I'm guessing they feel the same way after learning everything I told them about the former Ash, the SDRT, and the nearly deserted outside world.

"When are we going to get there?" a sleepy little girl asks her mom.

"Soon, honey. Just rest," the mom replies in a soothing tone, stroking the child's head.

I long for the days when my mother used to stroke my hair, and I could count on someone else to comfort me and make my worries fade away into dreams. But that's a big burden to place on someone else's shoulders, and even at such a young age, I could see the toll it took on my already worn-down parents. So I learned to soothe my own worries and fight my own battles. And they let me do It.

"Emery," Gina says, breaking into my reverie.

I look at her, and she seems to be struggling to say anything more. "Yes?" I encourage.

"Did you… Did you see Bretton Crandell in the Ash?" she asks, and I feel Eason go rigid next to me.

"Yes," I say, a little confused. "Haven't you seen him? Wasn't he with the others—the ones who stayed behind on the farm when everyone else was marching?"

She shakes her head. "No. Olivia and Rogan don't know what happened to him, either. They said he'd recently been injured and was confused. They expected him to be in his room, but when we went to look for him, he was gone, and the wall was smashed to bits."

"The antidote," I gasp.

"What?"

"It was the antidote that caused the barrier to expel me and the others. Bretton wasn't with us, but he'd had it, too. I just didn't think of it because he was hit by a poisoned dart—similar to the ones that hit Eason during the Gold Trial—and he became confused. We tried another dose of the antidote, but it didn't have any effect. I just assumed the barrier field would have passed right over him, just as it did everyone else who was under the influence of the Mind Mist."

"I see," mutters Gina in a controlled and measured tone.

"I'm so sorry," I whisper.

"It's not your fault," says Eason.

I don't respond. There's nothing else for any of us to say. After that, no one else in the truck says anything—not about Bretton, the Resistance, The City, or the uncomfortable jostling of the trip once we reach the end of the roads and have to travel over open land. The truck can't take the most direct route because of the dense trees near the farm, and going around adds time to the trip—time I fear we can't afford.

Again, I'm shocked by my own lack of foresight. Haven't I traversed the entire Safe Dome—Flame, Smoke, and Ash—on foot? So why does it surprise me how big it is and how long it takes to reach the edge? In my haste to return to The City and my desperation to save Eason, I had it in my mind that it would be quick and easy for people to flee the barrier field once it was down. But it's a long and slow process to move so many people so far. It turns out we're lucky Mara's being so slow about it.

Finally we roll to a stop. I peek out and immediately see with relief that the fire surrounding The City has been extinguished, a clear sign that the SDRT must be nearby, working tirelessly to free us. That must explain the delay. They wanted to make sure everyone could get out safely once the barrier field disappeared.

It must still be active, though, because so many people are congregated here, waiting and watching. They would have moved out if they could have. In fact, not far away I notice a woman throwing pebbles at the invisible barrier every few seconds, testing to see if they'll pass through or bounce back to her. I watch as she tosses another one and it ricochets off what appears to be open space and lands at her feet.

Still, I'm not discouraged. In fact, I couldn't have planned this better. I've rescued Eason, Gina tells me my family is somewhere among the thousands who have gathered here, and the fire is gone. Surely Mara will do her part soon, and we'll be able to leave this nightmare behind us.

I stumble from the back of the truck. My joints are stiff, so I walk around to stretch them. But after just a few steps the ground feels unsteady below me, and I stumble. My vision goes blurry for a moment. Soon I recover, but I don't for a minute think I'm truly fine. It must be the effects of the foreign DNA worming its way into my own—a reminder that time is running low.

"Careful there," says a man as he reaches out to me.

"Thanks." I turn to see that it's Doctor Hollen—Vander's dad—who's steadying me.

"Emery!" he says in surprise. "How did you get here? Where's Vander? Is he all right?" His questions come out in a flurry.

"It's a long story," I say, "but Vander's fine. He's in a city called Blue Haven where survivors have been gathering."

"That's great," he says with relief.

"Where's Van?" I ask, glancing around, expecting to see him nearby.

His face turns down. "We haven't seen him," he says. "Not since before the Refinement."

"What?"

"Gina said he made it to the Smoke through the tunnels," explains Doctor Hollen. "For a few days he was making runs for supplies from the Flame, but it's been several days since anyone has seen him." He's trying to appear strong, but it's obvious how concerned he is.

Behind us, Eason stifles a cry of pain as several people help him from the truck.

I know the doctor has plenty of his own worries, but I hope he won't mind if I ask for one more favor. "Can you help Eason?"

"What happened?" Doctor Hollen asks, instantly putting on a professional demeanor and jumping into action.

"Broken ribs," I say.

"Let's get him lying down here," Doctor Hollen directs, gesturing to a relatively flat piece of ground free of tree stumps and rocks.

I kneel at Eason's side and take his hand while Doctor Hollen examines his injuries. "You're going to be okay," I promise.

He nods, eyes closed and teeth gritted against the pain. I place my palm gently against his cheek and see him relax at my touch.

A gentle hand rests on my shoulder. "Emery," Gina whispers in my ear, "let the doctor work."

"I'm not leaving him," I protest.

"But we have a problem," she says.

I look up into her deeply lined face. "What?" I ask, wondering what could be more important than her son.

"The hoverplane is gone, and the barrier field remains in place."

CHAPTER 15

"What do you mean it's gone?" I say, stunned. I stand and back away from Eason, relinquishing him to Doctor Hollen's care.

"Follow me," says Gina.

While we walk, Liam spots me and runs over. The last time I saw him, I was handing him Curosene in the alley behind the Medical Center, trusting him to administer it to Whyle and save his life. When I left that night, I never expected to see him again.

"I heard you were back, Emery," he says with a smile. "I don't know how you managed that, but this isn't the first time you've done something everyone said was impossible." The obvious admiration in his tone makes me uncomfortable.

"It's a story for another time," is all I say.

He sticks by my side as we approach a small group in a tense huddle formation.

"Tell Emery what you saw," Gina commands, breaking through their whispered conversation.

They all turn to me, and among the faces I immediately recognize Cresta and Fox from my days on the farm in the Ash.

"Emery, it's good to see you," says Cresta, a gravity to her tone I never heard while she was under the influence of the Mind Mist. "Approximately two hours ago, we watched the hoverplane set down just over there." She points off toward the mountain. "It was forty-seven minutes ago that they finally managed to extinguish the fire surrounding The City. And seventeen minutes ago, they took back to the sky and left over the top of that ridge."

"We thought the barrier was supposed to be deactivated by now," says Fox. "We have everyone divided into groups and spread along the perimeter, but people are starting to wonder if this is going to happen at all. Can you tell us what's going on?"

Cresta and Fox talk as though they're leaders here, and Gina appears to be deferring to them at the moment. It seems strange until I remember Fox telling me that he and Cresta were two of the people who scored highest on the military tactics trial that occurred during their round of the Burning. Their ability to strategize and lead a group is probably why Ember wanted them out of The City to begin with, and why they've risen to command so quickly now.

I wish I had concrete answers for them, but I do know one thing: the SDRT wouldn't just abandon the operation that could be the catalyst for fulfilling their entire purpose.

"They'll be back," I say with conviction. "And we'd

better be ready."

*   *   *

Doctor Hollen gives Eason something that's supposed to heal his five broken ribs. While he's no longer in pain, when I check on him all he can do is pat my head and say, "So pretty," over and over. Doctor Hollen assures me it'll pass soon and he'll be good as new—not only his ribs, but all the bruises and injuries he sustained since his fake appointment to the Council. Still, there's nothing for me to do that can be of any help, and I don't even think he really knows I'm here, so I decide to let Eason rest.

"You need to sleep, too," says Liam. "You look like you're about to fall right over."

He's right about my unsteady gait, but that's just because everything I look at seems to jump and double and make buzzing noises. It disorients me. Sleep won't fix this, though. Only Curosene will help, and Doctor Hollen already told me he doesn't have any. That means I'm stuck like this until the SDRT returns.

So instead of staying with Eason or arguing about my need for sleep, I go searching for my family. As I walk along the barrier, I notice torches and movement in the darkness beyond the Safe Dome. While they keep their distance, I know who it is—Roamers watching and waiting. Until the SDRT returns, the barrier is our only protection against them and the disease raging in their decrepit bodies.

It's past midnight, and most people are starting to settle down for the night, clearing out rocks and twigs and hunkering down on the ground wherever they can find a place to rest. Every fifty yards or so, small fires give off light and warmth, but it's still difficult to make out faces as I stumble through the sea of people. I wouldn't be surprised if every single person in the Smoke has gathered on the outer edge in hopes of escaping The City tonight.

"Whyle," I call. A few people shoot me disapproving glances when my cries disturb their sleep, but I ignore them. "Brendon and Kinsley Kennish," I yell out my parents' names. "Whyle!"

I must go along this way for half a mile, stumbling and yelling until finally I hear my mom's voice.

"Emery?" she calls back to me in disbelief. She stands next to the nearest fire. Whyle and my dad are asleep on the ground near her feet. "Emery, is that you?"

"It's me, Mom."

I race to her as best I can, and she meets me halfway. She wraps her arms around me in a tight embrace, and I cling to her, breathing in the scent of her—a familiar mixture of flower soap and dust—and reveling in the feel of her cheek nestled against mine.

"I thought I'd never see you again," she says, her voice cracking. Tears moisten our cheeks, and I don't know if they're hers or mine, or maybe a mixture of both.

"How's Whyle?" I ask.

"He's fine," she says. "He's been great ever since the Medical Center finally got him some Curosene."

She doesn't seem to know how the Medical Center managed to come by that Curosene, so Liam must have kept my secret, just as he'd promised.

"I need to get back to Gina and Eason," I say.

"Gina and Eason Crandell?" she asks in surprise. She knows nothing of my relationship with Eason that developed since I last saw her. There's so much to tell her, but now's not the time.

"Yes. I want you all to come with me," I say, unable to bear being separated from my family any longer. I need to know that when it's time to leave, I'll have them with me.

"Whyle's asleep," she protests. "So is your dad. They've had a really long day."

"Mom, please. I have to go back, and I don't want to lose you guys again."

She seems to understand. Maybe she's scared of losing me, too. She nods and returns to the others. I want to follow, but I feel so weak, and I'm afraid if I try I'll end up stumbling right into the fire.

"Emery!" Whyle squeals the moment he sees me. "I thought you were gone. They said you couldn't come back." He runs to me and knocks me right over, tackling me in an enormous hug.

I laugh and hold him and kiss his head. I did this all for him, and I'd do it all again just to have him here with me like this. "Nothing could keep me away from you," I whisper back.

Then Dad's there. He pulls me up and hugs me, and the last missing piece of my heart clicks back into place.

Then a familiar, glorious sound fills the air—the growing roar of an approaching hoverplane.

"They're coming back!" I shout. "Everyone, wake up. It's almost time to go."

I feel the return of the plane like a million-ton weight being lifted from my shoulders. It doesn't matter that my head spins, that every sound beats painfully in my skull, and that I'm losing my ability to even stand, let alone walk. Help is here, and it's not up to me to rescue anyone anymore. I've done my part, and no matter what happens to me now, Whyle, Eason, and all of these people will be okay—better than okay. They'll be free.

CHAPTER 16

Together with my family, we race back to where Gina, Fox, and Cresta wait. Less than a hundred yards away, the hoverplane touches down on the ground and comes to a stop.

"Wow!" exclaims Whyle. "The other kids said it was cool, but it was gone by the time we got here."

"You'll get to ride in it soon," I promise.

"Really?"

I nod. Though, looking around, it's clear there are way too many people to fit on this single hoverplane at once. I've seen more hoverplanes fly over The City in the past week, so maybe they've called for some of them to join us, or maybe we'll have to make multiple trips. Either way, it doesn't matter. I feel so deliriously happy. Now that they're back, surely the barrier field will come down any second and we'll be safe at last.

"I'll be right back," I tell Whyle and my parents, and go to find Eason. He's asleep right where I left him. I press my lips to his cheek to rouse him.

When his eyes flutter open and rest on me, his face breaks into an enormous grin, beaming as though the sun has found a new home inside him. He raises a hand to stroke my face. "Emery, it's really you," he whispers. "I thought I just dreamed you, the way I've done so many times since you left."

"I'm really here, and you're safe now."

He sits up, wincing slightly.

'Are you in pain?'

"Only a little," he says. "It's fine." Then he pulls me to him and kisses me like he's never kissed me before—all heartache and hope and trying to hold on.

"Ahem," someone says nearby.

We break apart to see Liam standing there, looking both awkward and stricken. "People are getting off the plane," he says. "Gina wants you both to come."

We get to our feet, and Eason takes my hand. Together we walk back to the barrier's edge, where the hoverplane has landed just on the other side. At the sight of the plane, the Roamers recede into the shadows and disappear. Two people have exited the plane—Doctor Gill and General Rockshire. I pick up a pebble and toss it to test the barrier field, but it's still in place.

Doctor Gill's mouth moves as she speaks, but no sound reaches us here.

"I'll go out and see what's happening," I say.

"I'll go with you," says Eason, squeezing my hand tighter, and I can see in his face that being separated again so soon is more than he can bear. I'd rather not be separated from him, either. Besides, as much as I hate to admit it, it helps to have him steady me as I walk so the dizziness doesn't disorient me.

Hand-in-hand we breach the barrier field. I glance behind me to see the astonished faces of so many people, and at least a dozen who try and fail to follow us.

"Emery, you didn't get Curosene?" Doctor Gill says in concern.

"No, but don't worry about that. What's happening? Why hasn't Mara shut down the computer yet?"

"She tried," says General Rockshire. "But as soon as she established a link, she... Well, I'd say she passed out, but I don't know if that's the right term for a robot. Let's just say she shut down."

"What?" I whisper in horror.

"That's why we left," says Doctor Gill. "Commander Elben thinks he can fix her. He knows a bit about robots."

I'll bet, considering he's the creator of the first of Mara's kind. But I keep this thought to myself.

"He needed to get her to his lab back in Blue Haven," she says. "That's where they are now. If Commander Elben can fix her, this might still work. The real Mara back in Twelve is also working on the problem, to see if she can do anything through the main computer there."

"So what do we do?" I ask. "Just wait around and hope something happens?"

"We should give it a little longer," says General Rockshire.

"In the meantime, I was able to get more Curosene while we were in Blue Haven," says Doctor Gill, pulling a syringe from her bag. "You need to take this now, before the damage becomes too widespread." she steps forward, poised to inject me.

"Not yet," I say, pulling away.

"Emery, it's already been over eight hours since you injected yourself with DS10," protests Doctor Gill. "You must be feeling the effects. I don't think it's safe to wait."

"You said the monkey had twelve hours," I counter.

"Monkey?" says Eason. "Emery, what are you talking about?"

"Curosene will counteract the drug that made it possible for me to go through the barrier field, but I still have plenty of time," I say. "The monkey it was tested on lasted twelve hours."

"Lasted?" he repeats.

"Before it died," says Doctor Gill.

I feel Eason stiffen beside me.

"And that was one test on a different species," says Doctor Gill. "It's incredibly risky to assume it will be the exact same. I insist you take this." She holds up the syringe.

I look back to the concerned faces of my parents and Whyle's anxious and hopeful smile. I can't just leave them and hope it all works out.

And suddenly I realize that it's silly for me to even consider leaving them. I'm standing here with Eason, and if I could bring him through the barrier, I can bring them through as well.

"Give me a minute," I say, and drop Eason's hand.

"Where are you going?" Eason calls after me.

"I'll be right back," I promise.

I stumble back toward the waiting people, trying not to let my impairment show. To get through the barrier, I have to shove between the onlookers on the other side. I'm met with a cacophony of noise as hundreds of people shout questions at me.

"Whyle, Mom, Dad!" I find them in the crowd.

"What just happened?" Dad asks in amazement.

"I'm getting you out of here." I begin leading them toward the edge.

Gina catches up to me and grips my arm. "Emery, what's happening?"

"There was a problem, but they're still working on fixing it," I assure her. "Keep everyone here. I'll make sure they get the barrier down soon."

She doesn't look pleased with my answer, but there's really nothing she can do, so she simply nods and steps aside.

I take Whyle and Mom's hand. "Dad, take Mom's hand," I direct, wondering how long we can make this chain. I walk straight at the barrier and pass through effortlessly, bringing Whyle with me. However, Mom gets her head and one leg through and seems to get stuck.

"I can't move," she cries out anxiously.

"Dad, let go!" I yell, but he doesn't hear me. I open and close my fist over and over where he can see, hoping he'll understand, and finally he drops her hand. Then I'm able to pull her through with no more effort than it takes to break through the surface of water. As soon as she's through, I reach my arms back through the barrier and grab Dad's hand. Before I realize what's happened, someone else—a young curly-haired girl—grabs my other hand. I'm not sure if this is a good idea or not, but I pull them both through.

Then I look up to see the anxious faces of what must be the girl's parents. Though they look at each other from only feet apart, they might as well be separated by the entirety of space if that barrier field doesn't actually come down. I can't very well separate them, so I reach back and take both of them by the hands, and reunite them with their daughter.

General Rockshire is there, giving commands to the newcomers to stay together. He calls for guards from the plane, probably in case any of the nearby Roamers approach.

"Okay, that's enough," says Doctor Gill, holding out the syringe of Curosene.

Torn, I peer through the invisible barrier. I may have rescued the people who mean the most to me, but every face in the crowd is someone's Whyle or Eason, someone's mom or dad. I may only know a small number of them personally, but I know that I can't just abandon them any more than I can my own family.

"I'm okay for now," I insist.

I reach forward, and dozens of hands vie for my grasp. It feels so wrong to have to turn all but two away. But as soon as the woman and child they belong to are through, I instantly thrust my hands back out for the next pair.

The muscles of my arms begin to burn as they work, repeatedly pulling people through the barrier without a moment's rest, but I don't stop or even slow. I have to save as many people as possible while I'm still able.

"Emery, you need a break," Mom insists, but I just shake my head and keep going.

"Isn't there someone else that can do this?" Dad complains. "Give me this drug, and I'll do it."

"There's no more, and it'll take days to make more," Doctor Gill informs him.

There are still thousands of people waiting to be brought through the barrier, and my strength and awareness is faltering. I can't imagine I can save them all before I'm forced to take the Curosene. But even if Mara can't bring down the barrier, surely Doctor Gill can make more DS10 and rescuers can come for whoever remains.

As I bring people out, some want to stop and talk—to thank me and give me a hug, but Eason and General Rockshire move them along so I can keep going as quickly as possible. Hundreds of hands clench mine in captivity and release them in freedom.

I'm at the point of collapsing. I put forth my arms for what I'm sure will be the last time, and then I'll have to give up and let Doctor Gill fix my damaged DNA. Gina's not out yet, insisting on remaining behind with those who are left. Fox is here, organizing and directing people. From the inside of the Safe Dome, Cresta and Ollie take hold of my hands. I pull them through and then sink to the ground and vomit.

I can't even feel my arms anymore, but every part of my body I can still sense feels like it's enduring an endless internal battle between fire and ice.

"Emery," Eason exclaims. "Emery, are you okay?" He shakes me, and it feels like I'm being sawed in half.

I moan and whimper.

"I'm going to get Doctor Gill," he says, and rushes out of sight.

Cresta immediately takes his place. "Emery," she whispers. "How much longer until the barrier field is down?"

I shrug and shake my head.

"You're doing great," she says. "But I'm afraid it won't be enough."

"What do you mean?" I manage to say.

"We just got a message from Ember. She said if we haven't all returned to our work assignments by dawn, she's going to flood the Smoke and Ash with poisonous gas."

CHAPTER 17

"What about… What about the…mist… antidote?" My breath and words are coming in gasps.

Cresta shakes her head frantically. "The antidote the Resistance developed and the one Ollie and Roe gave us the morning of the march only protect our minds. Nothing can protect our bodies from poison."

By now, Eason has returned with Doctor Gill and General Rockshire. Cresta tells them what she already told me.

"Maybe you should have everyone who's left inside go back, and we'll return for them in a few days," says General Rockshire.

"That won't help," replies Cresta. "Ember said everyone. With the hundreds we already have out here not returning, it won't matter if the rest go back or not. She'll still gas the Smoke."

"Emery, here you go," says Doctor Gill in a soothing tone. "You're going to be just fine." She brings the needle to my arm.

Gathering every ounce of strength I can muster, I roll away from her. "No," I say. "Not until…everyone is out."

"But Emery," Doctor Gill, Eason, and my parents all protest.

"That will take so long," says Doctor Gill. "You could be dead before then."

"Then…stop arguing…and help me."

"Emery, honey, this isn't your responsibility," says Mom, her voice chiding and soothing all at once.

"It doesn't…matter," I stammer, forcing my lips to form the words. "I'm…doing this."

I get to my knees and crawl back to the barrier. I leave one hand on the ground to keep myself from flopping over. Then I reach the other hand forward and bring through a woman whose eyes brim with tears.

"Thank you," she whispers, and runs to embrace her son—a boy from Whyle's class at school.

"Here," says Eason, taking a seat on the ground behind me.

I lean into his chest, resting there and feeling steadied by the rhythm of his heart. He wraps his arms around me, gripping my arms and thrusting them through the barrier. Anxious hands take hold, and together, Eason and I bring them through.

Soon other people begin to gather, happy to have a way to help rather than standing around feeling frightened and powerless. They take turns holding and moving my arms. I'm offered sips of water and nibbles of food. A cool cloth is placed on my forehead. And others stand by offering words of encouragement. The effect of all our combined efforts is that we're bringing people out of The City at a rapid pace, and there's hope we might not have to mourn anyone's death after dawn.

Doctor Gill stands by, continually scanning me, and the lines on her face grow deeper with each passing moment. "Emery, I just don't think we can wait any longer," she finally says. "It's about to overtake your heart."

But I can see there aren't many people left, maybe fifty or so. Compared to the thousands behind me, this seems like so few. I open my mouth to insist we wait until everyone is out, but I can barely move my lips at all, and no sound comes out. I turn my head to look at Eason and see the terror in his eyes. I gaze back, begging him to understand that I can't just leave these people, no matter what it costs me.

He closes his eyes for one brief second and then takes a deep breath. "Work faster," he commands. "Emery wants everyone out."

And I'm so grateful that he understood, even if I can hear in his voice how badly this pains him. But I could never live with myself if I had to see the faces of the people I condemned to death every night in my dreams. I'd rather die than know I gave up on these people when I was their only hope.

The strange machine continues to churn—my arms being moved, hands clenching and unclenching, people escaping their prison.

I lose track of time. Everything is pain and confusion and fear. I think I see the first rays of sunlight streak across the horizon, but I don't know if that's real or not, because I also see stars blinking everywhere I turn. And then I lose the ability to feel anything at all.

* * *

I wish I could say that having my DNA morphed into something foreign—maybe plant, maybe rat, I'm not sure—is the worst experience I've ever had. But it pales in comparison to the complete, life-shattering agony of having your DNA sorted back out again.

I liked it better when I couldn't feel anything, but once Doctor Gill gives me the Curosene, I can sense everything in stark detail—all reds and bitterness and sharp edges and piercing noises. I scream and writhe, and she says she's giving me something for pain, but she either lies or it has no effect. Either way, I have no alternative but to endure every moment of the transformation in full awareness.

I keep my mouth closed, because every time I open it all I do is scream for someone to kill me. I mostly keep my eyes closed, too, because the lights in the Hospital Wing are too bright, but every time I open them, Eason's there next to me. He holds my hand and caresses my cheek and wipes away the sweat from my brow with a cool cloth. Sometimes someone is with him—Mom, Dad, Whyle, Ty, Gina, Tella. Then other faces start to rotate through—Vander, Kamella, Shawny. But always Eason, and I know I'm going to survive this.

Slowly it does get better, the pain receding into generalized stiffness, as though I worked a little extra hard on the repair crew the day before. Breathing no longer feels wrong, and I decide to ask the one question that has haunted me through these last hours.

"Eason," I moan, my voice weak.

He leans forward and places a hand gently on my face. "I'm here."

"Did we get everyone out?"

He smiles and nods, bringing his forehead down to rest against mine. "Yes, my mom thinks we cleared out the entire Smoke last night. You were amazing, Emery. You did it."

"*We* did it," I amend.

"You might have had some help, but it was you. You were the one at risk, and you were the one most determined to not give up. Everyone owes you—"

"What about the Flame?" I ask, cutting him off.

"What about it?" he asks.

"Are there plans to rescue the people there?"

"There's some debate about that," he says.

"What's to debate?"

"A few days ago, the computer gave everyone a choice to go to the Flame or the Smoke, gathering everyone who was willing to fight for and defend Ember into the Flame. There are those who are saying we should leave them alone. They had a choice, and they chose to side with the computer. Who are we to say they have to come out and change their lives?"

I can tell from his tone that he doesn't agree with this any more than I do. Sure, I'd love to keep people like Terrance Enberg locked up there forever, but what about Keya and Van? I don't think they made it out. One would think I would know for sure, but as I began to fade, I stopped seeing the faces or hearing the voices of the people fleeing the Safe Dome.

Before I can say anything else on the subject, the door to the little private medical room I've been placed in opens, and so many people flood in that I'm amazed they can all fit. It turns out a lot of people have been waiting to thank me, and it took two guards at the door to the Hospital Wing to hold them back until I was awake.

I spend the next hours saying the words, "You're welcome," so many times that my throat gets dry and my voice starts to crack. I receive more hugs than I probably have in my whole life, combined. It all makes me simultaneously happy and uncomfortable. I'm so glad to see all these people and to know that I had a role in bringing them to the safety of Blue Haven, which they already speak of so highly. But I don't merit their adoration that borders on worship. I only did what needed to be done. It just so happened that I was the only one who could do it, but that's not because I'm anything special. But it means so much to them, so I let them come one by one and say their thanks.

Slowly, my tide of visitors slows until only one or two flow in and out each hour. Finally, Vander and Kamella appear. There's something different about Kamella, but I can't quite put my finger on what it is.

"Oh, Emery," Kamella says, her voice like a familiar song. "I've been so worried about you."

"Did you see your parents?" I ask. I know they're out. They came through near the middle of the pack, and I was still lucid enough to realize who they were.

"Yes," she says with a grin. "Thank you for saving them."

I just shrug. "I'm glad you're back together." I finally realize what it is about Kamella that has changed. "Your hair looks amazing."

She smiles and runs a hand through the spiky locks that may be short, but look perfectly intentional and beautifully styled. The overall effect brings out her striking eyes and high cheekbones, making her appear older, more mature, and absolutely stunning. "A girl from The City did it. Her name is—"

"Petra," I guess.

"Yes. How did you know?"

"There was a time when she did magic with my hair, too."

In that moment, I feel almost completely happy…almost. But Vander has been standing back, not saying anything.

"Vander," I whisper, my voice suddenly hoarse. What can I say to him? We were in this together through so much. I was fighting for Eason and Whyle; he was fighting for his brother, Van. And now I have mine, and I've abandoned his.

"You look awful," he says.

"I feel fine."

"You're still a rotten liar," he replies with a sad smile.

"I'm so sorry…"

"Don't say anything that's going to embarrass yourself."

"I'm glad to see you're just as blazing awful as always," I mutter.

"I saw my sister, Amberlyn," he says. "I changed my mind—about when I said you were just as annoying as she is."

"Oh, yeah?" I ask, surprised.

"Yeah, you're about ten times worse, and she drives me crazy."

Eason's mouth and eyes have all narrowed into tight, angry lines, and Kamella jabs Vander in the ribs with her elbow.

"I missed you too, Vander," I say.

"Yeah, well, there's that, too," he says, and looks away, trying to hide the way he wipes his eyes with the backs of his hands, but no one is fooled.

Eason and Kamella relax.

"Vander, I heard how you helped Emery in the Ash," says Eason. "I wanted to thank you."

"I didn't do it for her, or you," says Vander.

"Thanks all the same," says Eason.

"Vander, I really am sorry about Van," I say in a rush. "I tried, but…"

He holds up a hand to stop me. "You did what you

could. Dad's working to convince the SDRT to make another rescue attempt. It looks like it might happen, but there are some other Safe Domes that are higher priority. It sounds like the situation in Three is getting out of hand, and after what happened in One…" He trails off.

"I thought they already deactivated One. Isn't that what they told us at that first meeting?" I ask, confused.

Vander rubs the back of his neck uneasily. "They did make it sound that way, and it's true that One no longer requires rescuing, but that's only because the people went crazy and all killed each other a few years ago."

"Killed each other?" I repeat in horror.

"Every last one of them," he confirms.

I'm not sure how to react to that. But if One was even more lawless than Two, where Keaton was from, then I can imagine how it might have gone that way. I wonder if that's how the computers were designed. Was it the Architect's intent to begin with utter anarchy in Safe Dome One, and slowly progress to more and more tyranny until it reached Twelve? Where everything was so controlled, even the slightest unpredictability was too much to be tolerated? Somehow in the process, the very essence of what it means to be human got lost, and the computer in Sanctuary couldn't see any reason to not just replace everyone with robots.

But if the purpose of the Safe Domes was just to shelter people from the ravages of the Withers, then what would be the purpose in making each Safe Dome so different, and so dangerous in its own way?

*   *   *

Several days pass while I recover in the Hospital Wing, during which time I'm almost never alone. All thirty-seven people who have fallen ill under the influence of the meal ration poison come here to be examined, medicated, and pronounced good as new.

The doctors from the Smoke are working with the Hospital Wing staff, and I overhear them say that they got all but three people out of the Medical Center. Those three were so far gone that it was unlikely they would even have survived the trip to The City's edge. Still, no one is happy to have lost them. That brings the death toll to twelve, including the three they left behind, among others. It doesn't include those still being affected in the Flame.

Doctor Gill complains that Whyle is her worst patient, but that's only because whenever she's not looking, he keeps leaving the exam table to come over and see if there's anything I need. I tell him I'm fine and to listen to the doctor, but he checks on me at least five times in an hour. It makes me smile.

"What caused their illness?" I ask Doctor Gill when she's finished treating everyone.

"It was a very specific toxin that bound to the brainstem and slowly cut off their vital functions."

"But why those people specifically?" I wonder.

She shrugs. "I wish I knew. The Resistance was right about it being in the food, and targeting people with a specific and rare recessive gene, but it'll take more research to venture a guess as to why."

Though this isn't a very satisfying answer, it's nice to at least know that it's over. It was Whyle falling victim to this illness that drove me to cross the Wall of Fire to begin with, and even though the last weeks have been nothing short of insanity and torture, it's over.

It's really over.

*   *   *

Someone opens the door to my hospital room in the dark and slowly creeps to my bedside. I don't pay the slow footsteps much attention. It's probably Eason returning from checking in on his mom. I roll over and try to drift back to sleep.

"Emery," whispers a low voice that's not Eason's.

I turn and squint through the dark to see who's in my room disturbing my sleep. "Toren?" I mutter in confusion. "What are you doing here?"

"I need to talk to you," he whispers.

"It's the middle of the night," I complain. "Come back tomorrow."

He ignores my protests and takes a seat next to me. "Listen, Emery. I've been doing some digging around here. Something isn't right with Blue Haven, or any of the new cities, for that matter. As far as I can tell, there are fifteen cities of survivors spread across the globe that house almost all of what's left of human civilization. It's the same computer that runs all of them—all connected somehow."

I sigh. "So, what's the problem?"

"Look, we were told that there's no crime in Blue Haven, that everyone's happy and has equal power through their little city interface things, right?"

"Yeah."

"Then why have I discovered at least twelve people who vanished after claiming to be the victims of crimes?"

"I don't know," I moan. "Toren, let me sleep." My eyes lids slide shut, blocking out the light and signaling to Toren it's time to leave.

He shakes my shoulder. "No, stay with me here. This is important. If I uncovered that in less than a week, you can bet it goes a lot deeper. I still can't figure out who's in charge of the computer. That's essential to know. Whoever controls the computer could control everything."

"And let me guess," I say with a yawn, "you think the Architect is controlling all the new cities."

"Elben? No. He's far too focused on these relic Safe Domes. No, it's someone else. Maybe General Rockshire, maybe someone I haven't met yet. But I need your help to figure it out."

"Why not go to Aiken? Haven't you known him a lot longer?"

"He's no use," Toren huffs. "Not since one of the communications staff helped him make contact with Mara back in Sanctuary. He just stays in his apartment and talks to her every chance he gets. But people trust you. They'll talk to you."

A profound fatigue settles over me that has nothing to do with the lateness of the hour or the fact that Toren roused me from sleep for this conversation.

"No, Toren," I say. "This isn't my problem. I've fought my fight, and I won. I'm done."

"But—"

"No, there's no conspiracy. Blue Haven is nice. And I'm just going to enjoy it here. Now please leave."

The overhead light clicks on.

"What's going on?" Eason demands, standing in the doorway.

"Toren came to talk, and now he's leaving," I say.

"Eason, you've got to listen to me," Toren pleads.

"I believe Emery said it's time for you to go," Eason says, holding the door open.

Discouraged, Toren disappears from my room.

Eason turns the light back out, and I drift easily back to sleep with him watching over me.

CHAPTER 18

After three full days pass—or four, counting the horrific first day when the only thing I was aware of was that I didn't want to be aware of anything anymore—Doctor Gill finally says I'm cleared to leave the Hospital Wing.

Doctor Gill escorts me off the hoverplane and into Blue Haven. "Integration Services will get you all settled in with a place to live and everything you need," she tells me. "But first, Commander Elben has requested that you visit him in his lab. He'd like the chance to talk to you about your experience in Ten." Then she calls a car for me.

I can't really explain it, but the prospect of being face-to-face with the Architect again is only slightly less intimidating than the prospect of facing off against Ember again—even without my superhuman immunity to barrier fields. But that's silly. He's just a man, and while he may be callous and egotistical, he has devoted his entire life to trying to save people—even if his initial attempts went horrifically wrong.

The car is small, with only one seat, and drives itself wherever you ask it to go. It zooms along the city streets so smoothly, stopping for pedestrians and taking turns with other cars at intersections. The ride is fun and relaxing, though my hands are still coated in a thin sheen of sweat when the car pulls to a stop five minutes later.

I'm deposited in front of a building that looks like a white cube. There are no windows. The only adornment or marking on the exterior is a handwritten sign haphazardly posted on the single front door, which reads: *Keep Out.*

I look around for any sign or confirmation that this is the correct location, but the car has already zipped off to pick up another passenger, and there's not another soul in sight. I have no idea where I am in Blue Haven, and it's not as though I have any way to contact Doctor Gill or call another car. That leaves me with little choice but to press through the uninviting door, which, incidentally, isn't locked.

The second I walk in, I realize the exterior must be so plain because once they got done with the interior, there wasn't anything left to use outside. The entire building is one cavernous room, and I wonder if there's a device or tool in existence that isn't here. Everything is neatly organized and seems to be oriented around one single focal point in the center of the room—a single metal table.

If I'm harboring any doubts about whether I'm in the right place, they're set to rest when my gaze settles on Mara lying lifeless on the table's sleek surface. She's unconscious, with half her robot head open to reveal her wiring. And in a chair next to the table sits a figure, slumped and snoring. He looks so relaxed that it takes me a moment to realize it's Commander Elben. Gently, I shake his shoulder to wake him.

He starts and looks around wildly, gripping the arms of his chair for support.

"I'm sorry," I say. "It's me, Emery."

He looks at me and blinks a few times, clearing away sleep from his vision. "Oh, it's you. Thank you for coming." He says it as though I had a choice.

"Doctor Gill said you wanted to speak with me," I reply, anxious to get this meeting over.

"Yes. Please, have a seat," he says, gesturing to the chair next to him. He looks so tired, with none of his usual arrogance, and my apprehensions melt away.

"Have you made any progress with Mara?" I ask.

"The robot? Yes, I'm quite close," he says. "In fact, in just a few more days the Safe Dome program will be complete, thanks to this robot."

"Really!" I say. "You think you can do more than stun the computers, but actually shut them down permanently?"

"Well, let me put it this way," he says with a wry grin. "In a few days, the SDRT will be completely obsolete and we'll all have to figure out something new to do with our lives."

My heart leaps with joy. I can't wait to tell Vander. No more rescue missions necessary. Finally, the Architect has found a way to regain control of his creations.

He leans back in his chair and gives a contented sigh. How heavily must the Safe Dome problem have weighed on him all these years? Perhaps all his arrogance is just his way of hiding the pain so he can get up and face each day.

"Did you know in the beginning that the computers would take over the way they have?" I ask. "Is that why you didn't enter one of the Safe Domes yourself?" It's not an accusation, just a question.

He shows no reaction to my words, and for a moment I think he's going to ignore the question. But then he sighs and surprises me by answering, "No, I didn't know." And while it's the only answer that exonerates him, he says it like the words taste bitter. It must be hard for him to admit what he didn't know—that his master creation took on a life of its own and left him in the dust, crawling behind and begging to regain control. "They were supposed to observe and guide. But in every case, they came to the conclusion that wasn't enough."

He stands and walks over to the table. He taps something in Mara's robot brain with a tiny metal rod. "I did intend to enter the final Safe Dome. But I couldn't right away I still had work to complete to make sure the computers would be stable, or else the barrier fields would be inconsistent and ineffective. But once the barrier fields went up, nobody was supposed to be able to enter the Safe Domes, to ensure their security. So I had an idea. I built a robotic replica of myself and placed it in Twelve. I programmed the barrier field to recognize my DNA and let me in when I was ready. Then I could deactivate and dispose of the robot, and no one would be the wiser."

"Why did you change your mind?"

"I didn't. Before I returned, the computer found the security breach in the barrier field and patched it, locking me out. I tried connecting and resetting it, but by then all the computers had shut off all communication to the outside world."

"So if you planned to enter Twelve yourself, you must not have known that it was going to start replacing everyone with robot copies."

He laughs. "No, of course not. What would be the point of that? Though it is a little flattering, I must say."

"How so?"

"The computer decided that the robot made in my image was a better specimen of a human than all the actual humans."

"But it's not human," I say.

"Yeah, well…" he mutters noncommittally.

"After all these years, you must have some idea of what went wrong," I say. Now that he's talking, I can't resist the opportunity to understand this thing that has literally been my entire world until just days ago.

"I have some suspicions," he says. "But in a few days, I'll have all the answers I've been looking for all these years."

He must mean once Mara deactivates the computers. I'm not sure how that will give him answers, but it's not like I know much of anything about computers.

"I heard you were successful in Ten," he says.

"Congratulations. I was told you spoke directly with the computer. Is that true?"

"Yes."

"And did she say anything to you?"

"She said lots of things," I say, confused. "Can you be more specific?"

"Oh, I don't know," he says as though he's just making idle chatter. "Anything that seemed odd or concerning to you?"

"Honestly, I found it quite concerning when she threatened to rip Eason Crandell's arms and legs from his body."

"Really? She said that?" he asks. "And Eason Crandell. Would that be the son of the councilman Bretton Crandell?"

"Yes," I confirm. "She's been torturing him for some time now, starting with the day he sent me to the Ash with that transmitter I told you about."

"Fascinating," he mutters, stroking his fingers through the thick stubble on his chin.

"That's not exactly how he would describe the experience."

He looks at me, his expression contrite. "No, of course not. Sorry, forgive my scientific interest in these events that I realize are very personal to you. I'm just so excited to see everything finally coming to a close. Emery, do you know what the greatest tragedy of the Withers pandemic was?"

I'm tempted to say the Safe Dome disaster that's still

not at an end, but I don't get the feeling that's where he's trying to take this conversation, so I just say, "No, what?"

"If the disease had been our only problem, it would have been a tragic blip on the roadmap of history, and soon forgotten," he says. "But it wasn't just the Withers we had to contend with. We also faced a far greater danger—panic."

"What do you mean?"

"Whole cities of millions were bombed to rubble, killing everyone whether or not they were sick, in a widespread effort to stop the spread of the disease."

I don't want to believe him, but I think of the city near Twelve that we flew over. I remember thinking it seemed impossible that nature could have decayed it so thoroughly in just a few decades. But if we turned it to dust and shards first, then it would fit perfectly.

"In other places," he goes on, "people feared the disease so greatly—probably because it appeared so grotesque—that they would kill anyone who came within twenty feet of them. People just seeking some simple help, who were no threat at all, were killed en masse. People who were sick couldn't get treatment. They were turned away from hospitals. Their own families abandoned them. Of course, we don't have numbers on this, but I would estimate that at least seventy percent of the people who officially died of the Withers really died of things like dehydration and starvation. They could have recovered if they'd had anyone to nurse them through the worst of it. Eighty percent of the Earth's population died in just over a decade, and most of it wasn't the disease at all. When it comes to the greatest tragedy in human history, it turns out, we did it to ourselves."

I stand completely frozen, unable to utter a single syllable.

"Don't get me wrong," he says. "The devastation would still have been catastrophic, but it's not nature we have to fear. Not really. It's humanity."

Slowly, my jumbled thoughts begin to coalesce into something tangible. I wonder why, exactly, he's telling me this. It seems pretty incriminating. "And you encouraged everyone to run away to your Safe Domes and abandon the sick?" I say, not sure if I should feel pity or disgust for him.

"They were going to run no matter what I did. I just gave them a destination and hope—and they were grateful."

"Less grateful now," I mutter.

"You're not seeing the bigger picture, Emery. I made everything that happened worth something. In centuries to come, people will look back on the Safe Dome experiment and realize that was the turning point between the barbaric before and the safe and serene after."

"What do you mean?"

"It's nothing for you to worry about now, but you can rest assured that your children will have a much brighter future than you could have ever dreamed was coming," he says, all the tension drained from his tone as though the conversation has taken a great toll on him. "Just a few more days, and it will all be over."

CHAPTER 19

"Mom, I can't find my other shoe," calls Whyle from the door of his bedroom.

"I'll help him," I offer. I leave my half-eaten breakfast and go to help Whyle. Just like back home in the Smoke, his room here looks like it was tumbled in a recycle sorter—but everything got mixed instead of sorted. "Whyle, we've only been here less than a week. How have you made such a mess?" I chide.

"It was pretty easy, really," he says with a smile.

I help him search for the misplaced shoe until I find it under a layer of dirty clothes. "Here you are. Now you'd better hurry so you won't be late for school."

"When are you going to get an assignment?" he asks.

I sigh. "It's not an assignment here. I have to choose on my own."

"So what are you waiting for?"

"It's a big decision, but I still have some time to think about it before I have to decide."

"Maybe you could work with Mom at a dress shop, or with Dad as a mechanic."

I shake my head. "I don't think either of those things are for me. I'll figure it out. I just need a few more days to think it over."

"And there's no rush," says Mom, standing in the doorway. "You've been through plenty to warrant a good rest. Now, let's get going Whyle. I'll drop you off at school."

Whyle gives me a squeeze and then races out the door. I'm so happy to see how well he seems to be adjusting to our new life here in Blue Haven. In fact, everyone seems to be thriving, just as Commander Elben promised.

Once the others have all gone for the morning, I'm alone, but their presence lingers in the way the kitchen chairs were left askew when everyone rose from the table, and Dad's books are piled by the comfiest chair in the living room, and Whyle's new toys spill out of his room. Integration Services offered me the choice of either my own apartment or moving back in with my family. The choice was easy. I fought too hard to get back to these people to have any desire for more separation.

I decide I might as well get things cleaned up. I start by gathering the laundry from Whyle's bedroom floor. Then I go to my own room. I don't normally leave my clothes strewn about the floor, but after finally getting released from the Hospital Wing, going through that strange meeting with Commander Elben, and spending hours at Integration Services, all I wanted to do when I got home was go straight to bed. I pick up the clothes I was wearing, and a yellowed piece of paper flutters to the floor.

I bend over to pick it up and realize that I'm holding

the note I took from Traeger Sterling's office in the Council Building. After leaving that neglected room, it never crossed my mind again. It feels odd holding it now, like touching a relic from a world that doesn't exist anymore. Even though The City is still there, I've moved on so completely that it seems silly to be worried about whatever Traeger might have written years ago.

Rather than reading it now, I put the note in my pocket. I'm meeting Eason later, and maybe we can read it together. It is addressed to his father, after all, and I did see Eason's name mentioned when I briefly skimmed the note's contents. Maybe he'll feel more interest than I do in knowing what it says. I just want to put The City, and everything related to it, far behind me as quickly as possible.

Soon, everyone can relegate the Safe Domes to mere memory. I wonder if Vander has been told how soon Commander Elben expects to have the Safe Domes deactivated. He'll want to know, so I send him a message on my city interface asking him to meet me at the landing zone this afternoon. That's the kind of good news that deserves to be delivered in person.

* * *

As Eason and I stroll through Blue Haven, I feel like I'm seeing it all with fresh eyes. When I was here briefly before, the world floated on currents of worry and uncertainty. But now, holding on to Eason as we walk the pristine streets and hear the birds chirping in the flowered trees, it feels magical and so right.

"I want to show you this amazing place to eat," I say. I head for the café Tella showed us on our first visit. I'm mentally running through all the foods I want Eason to try when we turn the corner and I walk straight into Liam, knocking us both to the ground.

"Hey," he complains.

Eason reaches out a hand to each of us to help us up. I accept, but Liam makes a point of getting to his feet unassisted.

"I'm so sorry, Liam. Are you okay?" I say.

"Fine," he mutters. He gives me a long, sad look. He opens his mouth like he's about to say something else, then glances at Eason and shuts it again. "See you, Emery," he finally says, and rushes off.

"That was weird," I mutter as he goes, feeling a little hurt. "I think he's one of the only people who never came to see me in the Hospital Wing. Do you think I did something to upset him?" I ask Eason.

He laughs.

"What's funny?" I demand.

"Do you remember when you thought Keya and I were something more than fellow Burn Masters?"

It takes me a minute to realize what he's implying. "You think Liam likes me and he's acting this way because…because he's jealous?"

He gives me a meaningful look.

"No," I say, in disbelief. "Just a few weeks ago, he

couldn't even remember my name."

"Didn't you say he was the one you went to when you returned to the Smoke during the Burning?"

"Well, yes, but it's just because he was working at the Medical Center and I thought I could trust him."

"And he did exactly what you asked, making sure Whyle got the Curosene, and kept your secret," he points out.

I can't argue that. And now I feel guilty, as though I've done something wrong. But I certainly didn't try to make him like me, if that's the case. If anything, I always tried to make people back in the Smoke want to leave me alone. And developing a crush on me was pretty stupid, since he never should have expected to see me again once I left for the Burning.

Of course, I harbored a crush on Eason for two whole years after he left, so who am I to judge?

I lead Eason into the cute little café with my mind still reeling.

Eason and I get steak, cheese-covered potatoes, and molten fudge cake to share.

Kamella and Petra are sitting together eating, apparently having sparked up a friendship after Petra rescued Kamella's hopeless hair. I wave to them, but choose a table where Eason and I can sit alone.

We eat in comfortable silence for a few minutes before I remember the letter I wanted to show him.

"Eason, I found something you might find interesting," I say.

"Really? Where?"

"Back in The City."

That visibly surprises him.

I reach in my pocket to retrieve the note, but before I can unfold it, Eason's city interface beeps. I wait as he looks down to read the message, and watch as his expression shifts from impassive to utter disbelief.

"What is it?" I ask.

"My dad," he stammers. "They found him outside The City."

"He's alive?" I shout, and jump to my feet. How is that possible after he must have been so badly banged up and burned, then left alone in the wild for nearly a week? "Where is he?"

"The hoverplane that found him is landing now. He's in their Hospital Wing."

"Let's go," I say.

"The message says that for safety, visitors are being limited to family only."

"For safety? What's that mean?" I ask.

He shrugs. "No idea, but I'd better go. I'll catch up with you later, okay?" Then he gives me a quick kiss and gets to his feet. He's about to leave when he suddenly pauses. "What was it you wanted to show me?"

I smile. "Don't worry about it. Go see your dad. He's missed you."

Alone, I take a few more bites of chocolate cake. I think about leaving, but I don't really have anywhere to go other than to wander back to my empty apartment. So

I decide to go ahead and see what Traeger Sterling was writing on possibly his last day in his Council office, before it was abandoned to fade under layers of mounting dust.

> *Bretton,*
>
> *I never thought I'd be saying this, but I need your help. I would go to Olivia or Rogan, but I don't know how willing they are to give up their control of the farm. You're the only one I know I can trust.*
>
> *What you never knew is that the central computer running The City is more than just a standard computer. It's an advanced A.I. which I named Ember. She is tasked with protecting the inhabitants of The City from whatever threatens them. I thought she knew best, and I executed all her instructions (including building the Wall of Fire and sending you to the Ash).*

I can't help cringing as I read Traeger's confession. It's a little late to finally come clean about all this. What good did he think it would do?

> *But recently I discovered something very disturbing. The Architect lied to us all. There was never a system in place to deactivate the*

barrier field. There was a transmitter which would send information directly to the Architect, but it didn't have a corresponding receiver, and had nothing to do with the barrier field generator. Regardless, Ember cut off those transmissions years ago. But as far as I can tell, the Architect meant to leave us here forever. What I don't understand yet is why.

I stare at the words, but my mind doesn't want to believe them. Maybe Traeger was mistaken. I may not personally like Commander Elben, but that doesn't mean he would purposely trap people inside the Safe Domes. I wish I could ask Traeger about this now, but Ollie told me he didn't survive the night when he was dumped out into the Ash. Apparently Ember hadn't been kind to him for many years, perhaps since she discovered he knew exactly the things he put on the paper I now hold in my hands.

My mind struggles to reconcile this information with everything I know. But it doesn't take long before I'm forced to at least consider the possibility that it's true. After all, wasn't it just yesterday that Elben called the Safe Domes an "experiment?" It hadn't made sense at the time, and doesn't fully make sense now, but it seems clear that he sees the entire situation very different than anyone else.

Is it possible he never meant to release the people inside, regardless of how the world outside changed? He did say he intended to join Twelve himself. But he also thought he had a way for him—and only him—to come and go as he pleased, so that doesn't really prove anything.

But Commander Elben said just yesterday that he was very close to deactivating the Safe Domes.

Or did he?

I try to recall his exact words. He said the Safe Dome program would be complete in a few days, and that the SDRT would be obsolete. But did he ever actually promise to bring down the barrier fields and free the people trapped inside? Or had he just finally gotten whatever information he was seeking in his "experiment," and is nearly ready to abandon what's left of it?

My stomach twists into uncomfortable knots. Instantly, I'm considering what this means, and how I can intervene.

But that's silly. There's a whole team that has devoted years of their lives to freeing the people in the Safe Domes. Certainly they can handle this. I should put this letter away—possibly destroy it—and never think of it again. I did my part. I saved Eason and my family, and so many others as well.

Haven't I done enough?

But I keep reading.

If we do nothing, we will be trapped here forever. Help isn't coming from the outside, and Ember will never let us go. Her entire mission is to protect us, and she believes the only way to do that is to keep us under her control.

I am monitored constantly, and can do very little despite my position. That is why I have sent word to Gina, and now you. You're the only people I can trust with this information. It is my hope that if both the Smoke and the Ash resist sufficiently, Ember will have no choice but to let us go. Though Gina has no idea it came from me, I've given her everything she needs to develop an antidote to the mind-altering agents used in the Ash. Hopefully she will have found a way to get this to you by the time the letter reaches you. If not, I can only pray that you'll be able to understand and do something.

With heaviest of heart, and sincere apologies,
Traeger Sterling

P.S. I was surprised to see Eason join the Burning last month. I assume he's following your instructions. Perhaps you laid out a plan to save The City long ago. Regardless, I will do whatever I can to assist him. I convinced Ember to assign him as Burn Master, where he will have high access and I will be able to offer any assistance possible.

When I finally tear my eyes away from the letter, my first instinct is to jump into action, but that was the old Emery—the one who had nothing and nobody to live for if she didn't find a way to save them herself. But I have everything, and if I'm not careful, I'll lose it all.

CHAPTER 20

Whatever may or may not be going on in the Safe Domes now isn't my problem any longer. I decide that my responsibility ends with passing along the information in the letter. After a brief debate, I settle on General Rockshire as the best option. I'll hand the letter over to him and let him sort it all out. I send him a quick message on my city interface asking where and when we can meet so I can give him an important document I found in The City.

Then I go back to enjoying my food and try to put the whole thing out of my head. Just as I'm finishing up my meal—the meal that was meant for Eason and me to share, and I'm so stuffed I can hardly move—my city interface beeps.

There's a message from General Rockshire: *Returned to Base Camp with Elben and robot. Will not be available to meet in Blue Haven until next week.*

My heart sinks. I was really hoping to hand off that letter as quickly as possible and put it out of my head. Elben said that what he's doing will only take a few more days, so presumably by the time General Rockshire returns, the Safe Domes will already be a thing of the past.

Unless...

I'm not going to actually do anything, but I could use some peace of mind. If I just knew that whatever Elben is doing with that Mara robot will actually lead to the Safe Domes' deactivation, then I could rest easy. I need to talk to Aiken. Or more specifically, the real Mara.

"Emery," says Kamella.

I turn to see her standing sheepishly nearby.

"Hi, Kamella." I look around to see that Petra has left and Kamella is alone.

"Can I talk to you about something?" she says, sounding nervous.

"I guess, but I was just about to go somewhere. Want to talk on the way?"

She nods.

We exit together and call for a car.

"Where's Vander?" I ask as we climb inside and start to zoom through the streets. This might be the first time I've seen them separated since we were picked up by the SDRT.

"He's with his family," she says, and then lapses back into silence, staring up at the sky.

"Have you seen Gar?" I ask, wondering why I'm the one doing most of the talking.

She smiles and nods enthusiastically. "Oh, yes. I visit with him every day. He's doing well, except he misses his parents a lot. But he's learning to speak, so that's really good."

"That's great," I say. We travel in silence for a few more blocks. "The ride is almost over," I finally say. "What did you want to talk about?"

"Can I ask you something?" she says, her expression equal parts distraught and uncertain.

"Sure, ask away."

"Be honest with me. Why do you think Vander hasn't kissed me?"

And I immediately regret my invitation. "Wait...what?" I stammer awkwardly.

"I've given Vander plenty of opportunities to kiss me, and I'm positive he wants to, but then he just...doesn't. Do you think something's wrong?"

"Um, I have no idea," I say, searching for a way out of this conversation. Discussing Vander and Kamella's love life wasn't something I'd *ever* hoped to do.

She sighs and rests her chin in her hands. "I just don't understand. I thought he liked me."

"I'm pretty certain he does," I assure her. He was obviously smitten with her from the moment he laid eyes on her in the forest of the Ash, and that only appears to have intensified over time.

She whimpers and drops her head mournfully into her hands.

I'm not good with this sort of thing, and I try to think of what I can say to wrap up this discussion without being rude.

Suddenly, her head snaps up as though the perfect solution has just occurred to her. "Emery, will you talk to him for me and find out what's wrong?" she says with so much hope that I find it impossible to flat-out refuse her the way I want to.

"I don't know about that," I hedge.

She takes hold of my arm. "Please, Emery. You're my best friend."

That takes me by surprise. How can I possibly be her best friend? But she seems so sincere that my heart breaks just a little for her. "What about Vander?"

"So you're my best friend, aside from Vander. But I obviously can't talk to him about this."

"No, I think he's exactly who you should talk to about this," I counter, trying to work my way out of this situation.

Her eyes glisten with tears that threaten to spill over. "Please, Emery."

I groan. "Ugh…fine, I'll see what I can do."

She squeals with delight and wraps me in an enormous hug.

I sigh. This is why I don't have many friends.

Thankfully we've arrived outside Aiken's building, so I escape before she can think of anything else to rope me into—like having a heart-to-heart with her parents to get them to work out their differences. Anyway, I'll worry about Kamella and Vander later—or maybe I'll put if off long enough that the stupid boy will just kiss her already, and I won't have to say anything.

According to my city interface, Aiken's apartment is on the tenth floor, so I go ahead and take the lift rather than running up all those flights of stairs. His building is laid out very similar to my own, and it doesn't take me long to locate his door. I pause before knocking, wondering if I should have let him know I was coming. But it's too late now. Besides, it doesn't sound like he's very busy these days, so I go ahead and rap on the door.

Then I wait, tapping my foot anxiously, but there's no answer.

I knock again. And again.

Finally the door opens a crack, and Aiken peeks out with squinted eyes and ruffled hair.

"Did I wake you?" I ask, surprised at his appearance.

"Yeah," he mumbles, reaching up to smooth down his hair, but it doesn't do much good.

"It's the middle of the day."

"Well, it's easiest for Mara and me to talk at night, so I've switched my sleeping schedule so I can stay up and talk to her," he says. "It's nice to finally get to speak directly to her. That robot wasn't a very reliable messenger. She kept telling me that Mara thought I was too clingy and if I needed anything I should just talk to Mara-bot because she's exactly the same. But I know my Mara wouldn't have said any of that."

I laugh because I can definitely imagine the Mara robot saying all of that in an attempt to garner more of Aiken's attention for herself and away from the real Mara. But Mara has to pass for her robot replica in Sanctuary, so she can't be sleeping all day the way Aiken is. "And when does Mara sleep?" I ask.

He looks guilty. "She's not sleeping as much as she should. I tell her to go to sleep, but she won't listen to me. She's never been one to listen to anyone." He sighs, a concerned look on his face.

"Listen, Aiken," I say. "I just learned something that might be a problem for the people still in the Safe Domes. I need to talk to Mara."

He glances back nervously over his shoulder. "Um, can you give me a minute?"

"This is important," I insist, pushing my way inside his apartment.

The instant I step past the door frame, I know why he wanted me to wait. Dirty dishes crusted with food cover the table, clothes are piled on the floor, and the air is saturated with a musty odor.

"How many days have you lived here?" I ask.

"I know it's a mess," he says, ashamed.

"No, honestly, I'm impressed. I thought my brother made a quick mess of his room, but I never imagined a disaster this big was possible in just five days."

"Four," he mutters. "It's just that in Sanctuary, there are processes for everything. Rules about how and when to do everything. Without that, I guess things kind of…get away from me."

"It doesn't matter," I say. "I didn't come here to inspect your housekeeping. I need to talk to Mara."

"Why?"

"Can you contact her? I'd rather not have to explain it twice."

He checks the time. "She'll still be with the Governor now, trying to stall his plans for more robot takeovers. We usually don't talk for another three hours or so."

"Please, just try," I say. "I have reason to believe that the SDRT is going to abandon the Safe Domes and everyone left inside. I hope I'm wrong, but I think Mara can tell me for sure, one way or the other."

That has his attention.

He pulls out a tablet, handling it carefully, and begins trying to connect with Mara. While I wait, I go ahead and move some of the soiled dishes to the return slot on his ReqMac to dispose of them. Just that one simple task improves the atmosphere dramatically.

"Mara, are you there?" he says, and I rush to his side.

"Yes, what is it?" a familiar voice whispers back. If I didn't know better, I would swear it's the same Mara I've known here.

"Mara, my name is Emery. I'm from Safe Dome Ten. I just discovered a letter with information that might affect everyone left in the Safe Domes."

There's a long pause. "Sorry, someone was walking by the closet I'm hiding in. It's not safe to talk now."

"That's what I told her," Aiken mutters.

"Give me a few minutes to find a safer place," she says.

The transmission ends.

"Seriously Emery, what's this all about?" he asks.

"I'll tell you when she calls back. But I did find out something else you might be interested to know." I tell him about Elben's plans to enter Twelve, and the robot he built as a placeholder.

"I knew it," he says, shaking his head. "Just one more way that idiot messed things up."

The tablet buzzes.

"Is that her?" I ask.

He nods and taps the screen to connect.

"Okay, what's so important?" she asks, getting straight to business. She's no longer whispering, so she must be somewhere she doesn't expect to be overheard.

"I found a letter written by one of the members of the Council in Ten." I don't waste time going into more details than that. Instead, I just read the letter aloud.

"Wait, so you're telling me there was never a way to let us out of the Safe Domes?" says Aiken, his face turning red.

"That's what Traeger believed. But the real question is what's happening now," I say. "Commander Elben claims that whatever he's doing with the Mara robot will lead to the end of the Safe Domes in the next few days. Mara, do you have any way to connect to your robot and find out what, exactly, he's doing with her and if it has any hope of actually freeing everyone still in the Safe Domes?"

"I'll try," she says. "Give me a minute."

We wait in expectant silence.

"Hmm," she murmurs.

"What?" Aiken and I exclaim in unison.

"There's a massive amount of data being transferred to her. It's as if… Hold on…"

I pace back and forth, nervously waiting for her to finish. What data could Elben possibly be using the robot to collect? And what does that have to do with freeing everyone still trapped in the Safe Domes?

"Tell me what you think this means," Mara finally says. "As far as I can tell, Mara-bot's connection to the Safe Dome computers is being used to copy the entire computer database from each of the twelve Safe Domes and save it in her memory banks."

"Will doing that shut down the computers?" asks Aiken. "Is she draining the information out of them or something?"

"No," says Mara. "It's just a copy. I doubt any of the computers are even aware it's happening. So the question is, what's he going to do with the data once he has it?"

"Whatever it is, I think it was the whole point of setting up the Safe Domes in the first place," I say. "Just yesterday, he called the Safe Domes an 'experiment' and said that the things we learn from them will change the course of human history."

"Okay, so maybe he's going to use the data they gathered to help people learn how to live better," says Mara. "You know, how to not repeat the mistakes of the past."

"Or force them to," I say, a terrifying realization forming in my mind.

"What?" asks Aiken.

"He said that the Withers wasn't what really killed most of Earth's population, but that people did it to each other because they panicked," I explain. "He claimed that humans are humanity's biggest threat."

"I'm not quite following," says Aiken.

"I'm saying, what if he's gathered all of this data so he can build—"

"The ultimate Safe Dome," says Mara with a gasp.

"Exactly. Combine the data from all the computers into one. Using everything they've learned by looking at people under very different but strategically designed conditions, he plans to create a new computer that can perfectly control everyone and eliminate the human threat."

"But who would join this new city after everything went so wrong with the Safe Domes?" Aiken asks.

I hold up my arm, revealing my city interface—the one that matches Aiken's and everyone else's in the Blue Haven. "I think we just did." And then another realization hits. "In fact, Toren said all the new cities are tied together by the same computer system. Once the Architect's newest program is inserted, there won't be anywhere left to escape to."

"I'm going to try and disconnect Mara-bot's link to the Safe Dome computers," says Mara. She goes quiet for so long I worry we've lost the connection, but then her voice is back. "I can't do it. I've been completely locked out."

"Have you made any more progress on deactivating the main computer in Sanctuary?" Aiken asks.

"No. In fact, without Mara-bot I'm back to square

one. It was her connection to the main computer I was going to use. Without that, I have no way to connect."

"Blazes," I exclaim. I wish there was one single time *ever* when things could just be easy.

"We should destroy the robot," says Aiken.

"It's not here anymore," I inform them. "General Rockshire told me earlier today that he and Elben took it to Base Camp."

"We might not have to destroy her," says Mara. "She needs the transmitters inside the computer's protective layers in order to connect."

"So that explains Sanctuary, with your tablet she connects to, and Ten, with the transmitter Emery delivered. But how is she connecting to all twelve computers?" asks Aiken.

"I wondered that myself," says Mara. "As far as I can tell, she found a way—or maybe the Architect found a way—to use the connection to a single computer to tap into the connection they all share. You see, even with the defensive signal-blocking layers they've all constructed, they can still communicate with each other. We tried tapping into that connection before, but couldn't do it. But it seems the Architect knew how to do it once he had a foot in the door, so to speak."

"So we need to shut the door," I say.

"Exactly," says Mara.

"Can someone tell me what you're talking about?" complains Aiken.

"I'll keep my tablet out of the Governor's House," says

Mara.

"And I'll get rid of Eason's transmitter," I say.

"The one that's in the heart of Safe Dome Ten?" says Aiken, incredulous.

"Exactly."

CHAPTER 21

I'm halfway to the lift when Aiken catches up with me. "Emery, stop. This is suicide."

"You want to see Mara again, don't you?" I say, still moving.

"I'll go with you, then," he says without missing a beat.

"No, Aiken, you've got to stay here. If anything goes wrong"—I don't mention how likely that is—"you and Mara are the only ones who know the truth and can do something about it."

He appears uncertain, and I don't have time to stand around and argue with him. "Aiken, Mara needs someone to come to when we get her out of Sanctuary."

"Okay," he finally agrees.

Just outside of Aiken's building, my city interface beeps, and I pause to check it. Eason is trying to contact me. That's perfect. He's exactly who I need to talk to right now. I tap the screen to connect.

"Emery," Eason says excitedly.

"Hi, Eason," I say, wondering how I'm going to tell him what I've just discovered or break the news that we have to go back to The City. But I know if I ask, he'll go with me.

"You'll never believe this," he says.

"What?" I ask, not sure I'm ready for any more unbelievable revelations.

"My dad—he's okay. He's doing really well, actually."

"How did he manage to survive?" I ask in surprise and relief.

"That's the part you'll never believe."

"Try me."

"Near The City, there was a group of Roamers living in a cave."

"I'm actually aware of that," I say, cringing at the memory and wondering what that could possibly have to do with Bretton being alive.

"They found him soon after he was expelled from The City. Fortunately, he'd managed to crawl away from the fire, but he still had some burns and several broken bones. They took care of him. Granted, their medical skills aren't the best, and Doctor Gill is doing surgery to fix several of the bones that were never set properly, but who can complain about that, under the circumstances?"

"They helped him?" I ask in astonishment. Suddenly, I can't help wondering if they'd meant to help me when we met? I was badly injured, too. Maybe they understood that I would find their appearance frightening, but were trying to make sure I got help anyway—injured as I was. Is it possible? And we thanked them by taking away their son, Gar. He certainly hadn't wanted to be rescued. Maybe we had it all wrong.

"Yes, they helped him. And here's the other interesting thing," says Eason. "Until now, the doctors thought it was only the children born to people who survived the Withers who were immune, and anyone else exposed to them without a mask or immediate decontamination treatment would contract the Withers. But my dad was with them for over a week, and he shows absolutely no signs of the virus. Of course, he's just one person, but it's enough to open up new research."

"That's really great," I say, wondering if I should ruin this moment by revealing what I've just learned. But I decide there's no point in that. I'll let him enjoy this happy reunion with his parents. After all their family has sacrificed, they deserve to be at peace for a while. "Are we still on for dinner?" I ask.

"Definitely. I'll see you then."

I can figure out a plan and break it to him then. Just a few seconds after we disconnect, my city interface beeps again. I think Eason must have thought of something else he wanted to say, but when I look down at the display, there's a message from Vander: Where the blazes are you?

I'd completely forgotten I asked Vander to meet me. I send back a quick message assuring him I'm on the way and call for a car.

Ten minutes later I'm walking across the concrete landing zone to where Vander stands impatiently waiting for me. Three hoverplanes are parked here today. The first one I recognize as the plane that picked us up. Bretton and Eason must be on one of the other two.

"About time," Vander complains when I walk up.

"Sorry. But trust me, what I've learned was worth the wait," I promise.

"Okay, what is it?"

I glance around to make sure there's no one nearby to overhear, and then I launch into a rapid explanation of everything, beginning with my meeting with Elben and ending with my half-formed plan to return to The City.

"So they're not going to rescue the others?" says Vander in disbelief.

"I don't think they were ever trying to rescue any of us," I say. "I think they picked up refugees just to gain more information from us, and to assuage any suspicions. But all along, they were just looking for a way to get the computer data."

"You really think they all know?" he asks.

I consider that. General Rockshire and Doctor Gill do seem to have good intentions. And then there are so many others, like Tella, who are just doing what they're told in service of a cause they believe in.

"No, I don't think it's all of them. Maybe it is just Elben, but what's it matter?"

"You're right—it doesn't matter who knew what. All that matters is that I'm going back to The City now to get my brother. And while I'm there, I'll destroy that transmitter, if I can," he says, and I can see the determination in his emerald eyes. He's still just as committed to saving his twin brother as he ever was.

For one blissful moment, I consider letting Vander go

on his own. Why not? He's still fighting for Van, and I have everyone I love right here in Blue Haven. Doesn't it make sense for me to stay and let someone else go off and fight the impossible battle this time?

But I know I can't do it, because the people I love aren't really safe—not yet. Safety is just an illusion until the Safe Dome computers are destroyed. And the first step is getting back into The City and destroying the transmitter that's linking the Architect to all the computers—the transmitter I put there. If I stay here and do nothing, and the world's cities fall under the tyranny of another of the Architect's programs, I'll never be able to forgive myself for that. And by then, there won't be anyone left to come to our rescue.

"We're going to need more DS10," I say.

Vander shakes his head. "There isn't any."

"How do you know?"

"Dad and I have been working with General Rockshire on plans to get back in The City. A few days ago, Elben cancelled the DS10 project. Doctor Gill was really mad about it, but Elben said it wouldn't be necessary anymore. Everyone assumed that was because he had a way to bring down the barrier fields using the robot, but now…"

"It's more likely he just plans to abandon them," I finish. "So without DS10, we're stuck."

"Hardly," says Vander. "After you cleared out the Smoke, Ember brought the barrier field in to just surround the Flame—probably to conserve energy. That means we can get in using the tunnels."

"Yes!" I exclaim. I start sorting through what to do next. Maybe I should contact General Rockshire again and tell him what I've learned. We'll need help to get back to The City, so we're going to have to trust someone.

Vander starts tapping his city interface.

"What are you doing?" I ask.

"Tella said anyone who wants to leave Blue Haven can request a plane. I'm putting that to the test," he says. A minute later, he claps and smiles so wide it looks like it must hurt. "The hoverplane will be here in ten minutes," he says triumphantly. "You can either come with me, or stay behind."

I stare off toward the three massive hoverplanes. On one of them, Eason is waiting for his father to wake from surgery—a father he hasn't seen since he was a baby. I can't ask him to leave right now. And I don't want to go without saying goodbye, not after we've been back together for such a short time. But if I tell him what I'm planning, he'll insist on coming, or he'll talk me out of it. He's probably the one person who could. If he took me in his arms and asked me to stay—to forget about everything else—could I really refuse him? It's always been easy to forget everything when I'm with him.

"I'm coming," I say.

I hope Eason will forgive me for missing our dinner date. And I hope my family will understand that it's for them that I'm boarding this tiny aircraft that's just arrived and returning to The City one final time.

CHAPTER 22

The small hoverplane carrying us bucks and sways in the wind, and I hold onto the sides of my seat, praying we'll stay aloft. The noise is thunderous as the wind whips around the little vehicle. While the large hoverplane of the SDRT was smooth, like a ship gliding through the air, this one bounces around wildly, and I'm certain we'll plummet to the ground at any moment. Inside, there's no room to walk around or do anything but sit. This isn't meant for long trips, just to ferry people from one stop to the next.

Somehow, we remain airborne until the orange glow of the Wall of Fire comes into view like an ominous beacon beckoning us—possibly to our destruction. The computer wouldn't accept Safe Dome Ten as a destination, so we told it to take us to Base Camp, knowing it would have to fly right past The City to get there.

I pry myself from my seat and carefully make my way over to where Vander crouches by the door. We both check our dive bands to make sure they're in place with the silver side out on all four limbs. Then Vander presses the button to open the door. The familiar glow of the

Wall of Fire dances not far in the distance. This is as close as we're going to get.

"Ready?" Vander asks.

I nod.

"Such a bad liar!" he yells over the roar of the engines and wailing wind, and he leaps from the plane.

I laugh because, of course, he's right. I'll never be ready to leap into the open sky. But I do it anyway, and quickly, because I don't want to land far from Vander and have to waste precious time trying to find each other again.

Once again, the first part of the descent is terrifying, and it feels like my stomach is in my throat, choking me. But soon gravity's pull is forced to ratchet down its power over me, and I land easily on my feet.

Vander has just come down a few yards away. "Blazes, that's awesome!"

My stomach does a back-flip and threatens to expel my lunch. "Agree to disagree."

Above, the hoverplane continues on its course to Base Camp without any clue that it has lost its passengers.

Even though we've landed in an area of what used to be the Ash that I'm not familiar with, the light coming off the Wall of Fire makes navigating to The City an easy endeavor. We take off at a brisk walk, wanting to get as far as we can before the sun sets.

"I can't believe they really abandoned the farm and all the recycle centers," I say. "How long do you think The Flame can survive on its own?"

"Who cares?" says Vander. "Isn't the whole point of coming back to find a way to end this? With any luck, it'll all be a thing of the past before the sun rises in the morning."

"Finding and destroying the transmitter will shut down Mara's link to the computers," I say. "But it won't destroy the computers themselves. We need a different plan for that."

"I've got a plan," he says. "Let's see that computer survive after the entire Council Building burns to the ground."

"Simple, but I guess it should work," I admit.

The walk through the empty Ash is eerie, and every shadow cast by the late afternoon sun makes me jump. I don't know if I'm more afraid of running into an Enforcer or a Roamer. But based on Bretton's experience, Roamers aren't really anything to fear, and no Enforcer will be outside the barrier field. Still, my nerves are wound too tight, and I need to distract myself before I do something stupid—like stomp on Vander's foot, thinking it's a snake, which I almost already did—twice.

"I should have brought some chocolate with me," I say, deciding food is a safe topic for distraction.

"Huh?" he mutters. "Oh, chocolate. Yeah, that would be good." He kicks a rock out of his path, his face turned down in a pout.

I know I'll probably regret this, but I go ahead and ask, "Is something wrong?"

"I shouldn't have left without saying something to

Kamella," he says. "I just didn't want to worry her, but maybe that wasn't the right call." I can hear his adoration and concern for her clinging to every word.

"Speaking of Kamella," I say, not because I really want to have this conversation, but because I'd rather have any conversation than think about what we're about to face. "I…um," I stammer, not sure how to broach the topic, and suddenly wish I hadn't even tried.

"What?"

I bite my lip.

He scowls. "I thought you liked Kamella now," he says, frustrated.

"I do," I assure him. *Or rather, I did until she asked me to have this conversation*, I mentally amend. "Honestly, she's one of the nicest people I've ever met. It kind of makes one wonder what she sees in you," I say, nudging his shoulder playfully.

He doesn't shove me away, which really shows the progress our friendship has made in the last few weeks. "Yeah, no kidding," he says. "Is that the problem? You don't think Kamella actually likes me?" He looks genuinely concerned. This nervous, unsure demeanor is a side of Vander I've never seen before.

"No, that's definitely not it. It's just that…" I take a deep breath. "She's wondering why you haven't kissed her," I say in a rush, the syllables coming out all mashed together as though they're all one big, giant word.

Vander stops walking, a stunned expression overtaking his features. That was clearly not what he expected me to say. Slowly, his lips part, bringing his mouth into the round shape of the word, "Oh."

"Well," I say, curious to hear the answer now that I've gone to the horrific trouble of asking the question, "you clearly like her—*a lot.*"

He runs his fingers through his hair, tousling it, and looks away. "I do like her. That's why I didn't want to mess things up."

"How would kissing her mess things up? She clearly likes you a lot, too," I say, still unsure what the problem is.

"It's just that… Well, I've never kissed a girl before," Vander admits with a huff.

"Really?" I ask, stunned. I hadn't given it much thought, but I realize now that I kind of just assumed Vander must have kissed lots of girls. He's certainly good looking enough to have had a horde of admirers.

I pull on his arm to get us walking again.

"Well, Van was dating Jessamine," he says. "I promised him I wouldn't kiss her, and she knew the difference between us, too. And I couldn't very well go around kissing other girls when I supposedly had a girlfriend."

"Oh," I say, surprised I never thought of that. "Wow, and you were okay with that?" I ask. "I mean, when you put it that way, it seems kind of selfish for Van and Jessamine to be together and leave you all alone, having to pretend to not be alone."

He shrugs. "It's fine. There wasn't really anyone I

wanted to be with. Not until Kamella. And now I just don't know what to do, and I don't want to ruin everything by getting it wrong," he says morosely, looking at me as though I might have the answer.

How did I end up in the position of relationship coach for these two? It's not like I'm any expert on love. I've kissed exactly one guy in my life, and the first time I did it, he disappeared afterward for two years without saying a single word to me first.

"I don't think there's much to get wrong," I say. "She just wants to know how you feel about her."

"And she wants me to kiss her?" he asks, smiling. "She told you that?"

I roll my eyes. "Yeah, she wants you to kiss her," I mutter. "Now let's never talk about this again, okay?"

"Deal," says Vander, but he's smiling the goofiest grin I've ever seen him wear.

Now we just have to survive long enough to get Vander back to Kamella.

That's when we reach the farm. We meander through the center of it, past the stables and animal pens, the dining hall, and dormitories. Everything is completely deserted. All the animals have been moved, and the fields of crops have been stripped bare.

"That explains why Ember was willing to abandon the farm," I say. "They picked it clean. They must have stockpiled enough to keep things running until they have more food growing in the Flame."

He nods.

There's no point in staying here, and neither of us wants to anyway. It feels like a shadow of something we used to know, and I half expect ghosts to be wandering such a deserted place.

From the farm, it's not long before we reach the ashen plain that surrounds the border of the Smoke. This is where the barrier between the Smoke and Ash rested until very recently. But when we reach the dividing line—ash on one side, broken concrete on the other—we find with relief that there's nothing to impede our progress. If the barrier field was in place here, I have no idea what we'd do next. Fortunately, Vander's information about the barrier field being moved all the way back to the Flame appears to be accurate.

"Are you up for a run?" I ask. "I'm ready to get this thing over with, and I want to get there while it's still light."

"Me too," he says. "The Smoke's your territory. You lead the way."

He does a good job of keeping up, and we run all the way through the empty streets lined with dilapidated houses, recycle centers, and never-ending dirt. Once we reach the Nutrition Station where I used to eat my meals, we're close to the Wall of Fire, and I bring us to a stop to rest at one of the outdoor tables.

Suddenly, a harried sound escapes my lips that's half frenzied laugh and half whimper.

"What could possibly be funny right now?" he asks, his eyes darting between me and the ominous barricade nearby.

"I just realized that this is the exact same table where my brother was sitting the morning he got sick. If that hadn't happened, or if I hadn't chosen to cross the Wall of Fire to find Curosene, maybe none of this would have ever happened."

He rolls his eyes. "Yes, everything is definitely your fault. It had nothing to do with the Architect, or a demon computer system, or Eason, or anyone else. Don't take this the wrong way, but honestly, isn't that a little conceited to think it's all because of you?"

"Okay, it was all happening anyway," I admit. "But if I hadn't joined the Burning when I did, Eason would have kept waiting for someone from the Smoke to come. He was waiting for an ally. So maybe it was all inevitable eventually, but would any of it have happened now?"

He shrugs. "Maybe not. But does putting it off make it any better? The way I see it, if we hadn't gotten out when we did, Elben would have still found a way to download all the computer data and start his little nightmare utopia, and we'd all be stuck in the Safe Dome forever—or until things went the way of One and we all ended up killing each other."

I consider his point. "You're probably right. I guess that makes me feel a little better."

"Great. Now are we going to get on with this, or just wait here until Ember notices us and sends a horde of Enforcers out to get us?"

"I'm ready to get moving," I say. "The only tunnel I

know leads between the school and the Burning Center. Do you know of a better option?"

The tunnels are really Vander's expertise. It was his mom who knew about them because her father had been the mayor of the town the Safe Dome was built on top of. Vander and his brother have used the tunnels all their lives to aid them switching places and hiding the fact that they're actually two separate people.

"There's one that runs from the Justice Building on this side all the way to the Council Building," he says. "It's not one I ever used because both of those were places Van and I tried to steer clear of, but I remember it was on the map."

"That sounds like exactly what we need," I agree. "The Justice Building is just a few blocks this way. Ready?"

He stands, slowly blowing out a deep breath, and nods. "Ready as I'll ever be."

* * *

We have to break a window to get into the deserted Justice Building, but once we're inside, it's easy enough to find the tunnel entry below the wooden floorboards.

"You want to go first?" Vander asks as we kneel next to the dark, dank opening.

"You know the tunnels better. Maybe you should."

He shrugs and lowers himself inside. Once he's scurried in far enough, I follow. Traveling through the tunnels is one of my least favorite experiences. I feel as though the earth has swallowed me and is slowly working me through its snakelike body. I feel as though the cold darkness could go on indefinitely, and whether I go forward or backward, I could be trapped down here forever.

"Count your breaths," Vander says after we've traveled long enough that I've lost track of time.

"Huh?"

"It can be hard to stay focused down here," he says. "Count your breaths. It'll keep you from panicking."

"I wasn't about to panic," I say, but the breathless quality to my words betrays me.

"Suit yourself," he mutters.

Silently, I begin counting my breaths.

One hundred and eighty-three breaths later, Vander comes to a sudden stop. "Blazes!" he cries. "No, no!"

"What is it?"

"We're almost at the end, but the tunnel is blocked by a barrier field," he says.

"What? Let me see."

He squishes to the side of the tunnel to let me crawl past him. Our way can't be blocked. If it is, I really might just lose my mind. I put my hand out and feel along carefully in front of us, but there's nothing there.

"Vander, there's no barrier field," I say, crawling forward.

"Yes there is," he insists. "I know I felt it."

"I don't know what you think you felt, but it's wide open," I say. "Come on."

I crawl along with Vander muttering something behind me. And in just a few more yards, I run into the point where the tunnel curves back upward to a wooden plank above. I stand up, pressing against the exit with my shoulders, and it gives way easier than I would have expected.

"We're out," I whisper. I pull myself up and find that we're in some kind of storage room filled with shelves and shelves of boxes. The air is so dusty that I doubt anyone has been in here in years. Our next challenge will be getting out of here and up to the second floor, back to Traeger's office where I hid the transmitter in a drawer.

Vander emerges from the tunnel and gets to his feet, brushing the dirt from his knees and coughing from the dust our entrance has thrown into the air.

I figure it's too much to hope that the door will simply be unlocked, but I decide it's at least worth a try before we attempt any more drastic measures. But just as I put my hand on the knob to test it, I'm thrown back as seven Enforcers burst through the door brandishing blasters.

CHAPTER 23

In the lead is Terrance Enberg, his lips curling into a hideous smile. "Emery Kennish. I've never met anyone so averse to their own self-interest," he says. "If you've got a death wish, I can just shoot you right now."

"I'm pretty sure Ember wouldn't be happy about that," I say, and I can see in the way his eye twitches when I mention her name that I'm right. She wants me alive. She wants answers that can't be gotten any other way. "I'm sure you're here to take us to her, so let's get on with it."

Vander shoots me a look like I'm crazy, and I'm not entirely sure where my bold response has come from, but I feel certain that this is all inevitable somehow. One way or another, this story was always leading to one last meeting between Ember and me. We might as well get it over with.

The team of Enforcers surrounds us and leads us from the storage room. As we march along, I keep glancing at the Enforcer to my right. She looks so familiar. Then I realize that she's shaved off her long, black hair, but her nose is still as pinched as ever.

"Mieka," I whisper. "What are you doing here?"

She scowls at me. I can feel that any friendship that may have developed between us in the Ash has evaporated, and she hates me just as much now as she did when I was just the girl from the Smoke in the Burning.

"I came back to the Flame when Ember made the offer. They made me an Enforcer," she says smugly. I can imagine that's probably the assignment she was hoping for back in the Burning. Still, why would anyone want to help Ember after all we've seen?

"Why are you fighting for The City, and Ember? You've seen how cruel she is. You've seen the Mind Mist that controls everyone."

"Shut up," she hisses in her most menacing tone. "You're the one who ruined everything. Life was finally good on the farm. For once in my life I was happy, and you're the one who destroyed that."

I'm shocked. "You liked the Mind Mist?" I ask in disbelief.

"What's not to like? Every day was just…calm."

"No more talking," Terrance barks.

I mull over her words. Is it possible that some of these people truly don't want to be rescued? They'd rather give up all freedom just to be shielded from their own unpleasant thoughts and fears? Rather live their lives controlled by a computer program just so they don't have to decide anything for themselves?

Our footsteps echo in the long empty hallway, announcing our approach to the door at the end of the first-floor corridor—the room where I last faced Ember. But before we reach it, we're brought to a halt in front of another door.

Terrance opens it. Then he grabs Vander roughly by the shirt collar and drags him forward. "Ember's only interested in the girl," he says, and shoves Vander roughly inside. "We've got a special treat for you," he adds with a sneer.

The clank of the slamming door echoes down the hallway, but is quickly replaced with the sound of Vander's cries; they have a haunted quality to them I can't quite define.

I inhale sharply, fighting the urge to scream or lunge for the door or show any reaction at all. None of that will do any good. The only way I can save Vander now is to face Ember and find a way to walk away alive. If I fail in that, it'll cost Vander his life, too. Of that I'm certain.

We resume our march down the hallway, and it feels so much colder and darker without Vander by my side. I hadn't counted on having to do this alone, and I'm not sure I'm strong enough.

Terrance opens the door, and Ember's ethereal form is standing in the middle of the empty room, her crimson red lips curved into a smile that doesn't touch her eyes.

"Emery Kennish, what a surprise. Not many people manage to surprise me. Certainly not more than once. But you just keep doing it."

From the corner of my eye, I see Terrance motion for the Enforcers to follow him out the door.

"No, Terrance," says Ember. "This time you stay."

I guess she learned from her mistake last time, and isn't taking chances now.

Terrance's mouth contorts into a twisted smile, and he takes up a post near the door. The other six Enforcers fall into formation, lining the wall next to him on either side.

She slowly steps toward me until she stands so close that I should be able to feel her breath on my face, but there's nothing but eerie stillness. I'm not sure what she means to do until suddenly, so fast I don't see it coming, she slaps a hand across my face so hard that my vision goes black and my ears ring as I'm thrown to the ground. One small patch at a time, the world becomes visible again. When I look up, I see actual shock on Ember's pale face.

"I wasn't expecting that," she admits. "You've surprised me once again. Tell me, what is it that you felt was important enough to risk coming here without your ability to move through barrier fields, even though the likelihood that I will kill you is"—her entire body freezes unnaturally for a fraction of a second—"ninety-nine point seven percent."

I notice that she calculates my odds of survival as point two percent higher than the last time we met. I take that as an encouraging sign. My head is still ringing like a bell, but I can't wait around to recover. Shakily, I force myself to stand.

"I assume you don't want me to hit you again, or to harm your friend we have in the other room," she says.

"So explain to me exactly how you did that little trick with the barrier fields."

"I will," I promise. "But first, I have a question." I know her desperation for that information is the only weapon I wield against her, and I must be careful and deliberate with it.

"Just one?" she says.

"For starters. What do you believe is the biggest threat to the safety of humanity?"

"That's simple. The biggest risk to humans' safety is humans themselves. They must be protected from their own destructive instincts." Suddenly an ornate chair appears behind her, and she sits as though on a throne.

"But was it humans who poisoned the food here in The City?" I ask.

"That was necessary. The people possessing the P71-M gene are a danger to the rest of the population," she says without any hint of remorse.

I'd thought I could do this calmly, but suddenly, everything takes on a reddish hue that has nothing to do with the hit I just sustained and everything to do with the rage that's seized me. "My brother isn't a threat," I yell. "He's an innocent, eight-year-old boy. He never hurt anyone."

She's unfazed by my outburst. "I have identified a potential danger. A new disease outbreak is likely to occur. I must remove those who have the genes to be carriers in order to protect the rest," she explains with mechanical detachment, like an engineer speaking of removing a defective wire from an engine.

"So they have a disease that you're trying to keep from spreading?" I ask, concerned. Could Doctor Gill have missed that on their exams?

"Not yet, but the probability of its development grew to an unacceptable level. Once its likelihood surpassed fifty-one percent, I had no choice but to intervene."

"You always have a choice," I reply.

She looks at me as though I've said something completely incomprehensible.

I try a different approach. "So instead of a fifty-one percent possibility they would die, you made it a one hundred percent certainty. What if it never happened?"

"The risk to the greater population was unacceptable."

"So why not just exile them from the Safe Dome the way you did to me?"

"The risk is too high. My first priority is the humans inside The City, but I can't knowingly endanger those outside it, either. The only safe solution is to eliminate them."

This is going all wrong. I need to remain calm, to think clearly and logically. I have to make her understand, and I can't do that if my mind is swimming in fury and fear. I think of Eason, how confident and controlled he always appeared, even though he knew all along what was at stake. I can do that, too.

"I can see that you really do care about humans," I say, forcing my features into a placid mask.

She nods in approval. "Of course I do. The

preservation of humans is my sole purpose for existence."

"And if something threatens humans' ability to survive and thrive, wouldn't you be obligated to destroy it?"

"Absolutely. I would have no choice, which is why I will kill you very soon."

As much as I hate her response and the cold, detached way she promises my death, I suddenly realize I've already won—she just doesn't know it yet. And all the anger and fear clawing at my insides melts away.

"What if I could show you a greater threat to humanity than me or a disease—greater than all of humanity combined? What would you do?" I say.

"I would do anything in my power to eliminate the threat," she says. "But there cannot possibly be a bigger threat to humans than they pose to themselves. Your species had its chance to determine its own course, and it nearly destroyed itself. Humans proved to be more destructive to themselves than all other forces of nature combined."

"You're right. We got it horribly wrong. But it wasn't all humans that did that. It only takes one to drop a bomb, leveling a city and wiping out millions. Only a few to spread rumors, lies, and fear that cause people to panic. You called me an outlier when we last met because I wouldn't give up despite everything you've done to subdue me. But I think a lot more people are like me than you think, and a lot more would be if given half a chance. And if you want humanity to survive, that's what we need—more people who cling to what it truly means to be human."

She stands and stalks slowly toward me. "You want to lecture me about what it means to be human? I have watched over your kind since before you were born."

"But that's not the same as understanding us," I say, my voice trembling. "I'm only alive today because I refused to give up hope when all logic said I should, and because I found a way to trust even when your society taught me never to do that."

She reaches out and places a cold hand around my throat, squeezing just hard enough that I can barely breathe, but her threat is clear. "Tell me how you did it!" she hisses.

"I don't know…how I found the courage," I gasp, struggling for air. "But if more people had those…qualities back in the early days of the…Withers, how many billions of lives would…have…been…saved?"

She freezes, and I wait for her to finish whatever she's calculating as I gasp for air through her statuesque hold on my neck. "I'm not able to calculate that figure. There are too many missing data points," she finally says.

I fall away from her, holding my throat and gasping for air, but I keep talking while I have the chance. "I can't give you that number, either. But I can give you names— names of real people who would be dead right now if it weren't for someone defying the structure you tried to impose. Whyle Kennish, Vander Hollen, Kenna…"

"That's enough," growls Terrance.

Ember bends down and grabs my hair, using it as

leverage to pull me back up to my feet, forcing me to look her in the eyes. "You're stalling. Give me the information I need so that I can eliminate you as a threat once and for all."

"How many people are dead who wouldn't be, were it not for your efforts to protect humanity?" I spit the words at her, and while she may not have welcomed the question, she freezes, unable to prevent herself from running the calculations. I don't know if she's listening or if my words will sway her now, but others in the room are listening, and maybe I can sway them, so I begin listing names, "Alexia Hayworth, Traeger Sterling, dozens—or maybe hundreds—of third babies. Dozens of people killed by the meal rations."

Ember falls back a step and goes rigid, struggling to calculate so many possibilities and uncertainties. "That isn't a number I can compute," she finally says, her voice carrying a note of concern for the first time.

"And what about all the people who might rather be dead because their lives aren't their own at all?" I throw at her, forcing her back into her frozen state. "Most of the people from the Smoke, Keya, Petra, and Mieka."

As I say her name, I steal a glance at Mieka from the corner of my eye. She looks away, but not before I see the tears rolling down her cheeks.

"I said, enough," hisses Terrance, bringing his blaster up and pressing the tip into my chest.

But Ember is still a statue, and I know without her approval he won't fire, so I keep talking.

"You're right about humans being dangerous, but it's the kind of humans who try to control and manipulate others who are the greatest danger. They are followed closely by the people who let them, the people who welcome someone telling them what to do every moment of every day and never question, and slowly each day become less and less human."

I stand straighter, certainty of my victory growing with each word I pronounce. "There are very few people who are true dangers to the world. And when the rest of us step aside and hand them power, that's when humanity is doomed. But in order for humans to have the strength to stand up to those threats, they have to have a chance to try, and to have hope that they might succeed. They have to find people to trust, and be free to take action. The Safe Domes were calculated to destroy the very characteristics that make us capable of protecting ourselves."

"I said stop talking!" yells Terrance. "Ember, let me shoot her."

But the personified form of the computer is still frozen. I wonder if maybe Mara found a way to tap in and is dismantling her at this very moment. I still don't know if Ember can hear me, but Mieka can, and so can the others in the room, so I keep talking.

"Can't you see the flaw in the Safe Dome program now? In an effort to protect people, they each target and seek to destroy some element of what it is to be human that we most need in order to protect ourselves. The

Architect always knew that the Safe Domes were flawed. If he told you otherwise, he lied. And now he's linked in to all twelve Safe Dome computers and is downloading a copy of your entire database."

At this, Ember's head whips from side to side as though she's looking for something.

"And when he has all the data, he's going to use it to create a new program to entrap and enslave people—to squash from them all that is truly human for generations to come. I don't know if people will ever be able to break free if he's allowed to succeed."

Ember rolls her head back around to face me and freezes, her eyes glazing over like frosted marbles.

"What have you done?" Terrance yells, becoming completely unhinged, and I feel certain he's going to shoot me—going to kill me—without Ember's order. I'm expecting it so much so that I don't even flinch when the low whine of the blaster's kill shot reverberates off the concrete walls.

CHAPTER 24

What I don't expect is to still be standing, or to watch Terrance slump to the ground beside me. I look around in surprise to see not one, but three Enforcers—Mieka included—with blasters raised, all pointed at Terrance. Did they all fire, or just one? I don't know, and it doesn't matter.

I turn back to Ember, who looks down at the dead chief Enforcer. "I see," she whispers.

We all wait with bated breath to find out what exactly she's come to understand.

A whole minute passes, and no one moves—least of all Ember.

Then a second minute ticks by, and nothing happens.

I consider that this might be my only opportunity to run and escape this place. I suspect I'll have at least three allies if I try. I've done what I can, and maybe I can still get out of here alive—maybe even save Vander if I hurry.

But before I move, Ember snaps back to life. She stands and steps slowly toward me, reaching out her arms. I brace myself, my face and neck still stinging from her assault, but she brings her hands to rest gently on my shoulders. "I miscalculated. Humanity needs more outliers."

And then she disappears.

"What…just happened?" stammers one of the Enforcers who raised a blaster in my defense against Terrance.

"I think I broke Ember," I say, not daring to truly believe it myself.

It's not just the ghostly form of Ember that's gone, but also the chair she sat on.

Then an unexpected clinking fills the room as all the Enforcers' intercuffs deactivate, snap open, and fall to the floor.

I turn and run from the room, and no one makes a single move to stop me. Maybe this is a trick, or maybe Ember is really gone—self-destructed as her last act to protect the people of this Safe Dome. Either way, I still need to destroy the transmitter. I have to be certain the Architect can't get any more data from any of the twelve computers.

A cloud of dust greets me as I throw open the unlocked door to Traeger's office. Coughing, I cross the room and pull open the desk drawer where I stashed the small silver sphere, and a yellow light illuminates the small space indicating that the transmitter is active. I throw the little device to the ground with all the force I can muster, hoping to see it shatter, but it bounces and rolls away, the light still blinking.

I retrieve it; it's dented, but still apparently operational.

"Need some help?" Mieka asks from the doorway.

I smile. "Want to fire that blaster one more time?"

She pulls the weapon from her shoulder. "Love to."

I set the transmitter down on the desk chair and step out of the way.

Mieka takes aim, pulls the trigger, and the Architect's connection to his evil creations evaporates into dust and smoke.

"Nice shot," I praise as I run past her and exit the room.

Bounding down the stairs, I race back to the room where Vander was imprisoned. The Enforcers that were my guards in Ember's presence now watch on with stunned and confused expressions. As I approach my goal, I can hear the gut-wrenching sound of screams and scuffles inside. Without hesitating, I pull on the door and it swings open easily.

Vander and a thin, wiry Enforcer are tangled in a wrestling match on the ground. It's impossible to discern who's winning the fight, as both of them are coated in sweat and blood. I wonder why the Enforcer didn't just blast him, but as I rush forward, my feet trip over the broken pieces of the Enforcer's weapon. Impressed, I pause for only the briefest moment. That's a story I'm going to have to get from Vander—but later. First, I have to make sure Vander makes it out of here alive. Apparently, this Enforcer didn't get the message that the fight is over. Did he even notice when his intercuff deactivated and fell to the ground?

I leap at the Enforcer's back, gripping both an arm and a thick lock of hair, and yank backward as hard as I can. My efforts are enough to give Vander the upper hand, and he twists free of the choke hold he's been locked in. With a swift motion, he sends a nicely aimed kick right into the Enforcer's nose.

I can't help noticing the handful of peering eyes in the doorway—Enforcers watching who don't bother to lend a hand, or a blaster, to save Vander. But at least they don't assist their fellow officer, either. I imagine they don't know whose side to take anymore, now that the lines aren't drawn so neatly for them.

The Enforcer's head bobs several times as he fights for consciousness. Together, Vander and I grab him by the arms, and shove him toward the door. The others in matching uniforms receive him and drag his barely-conscious body away, presumably for medical attention.

I'm expecting to follow them out of this place, leave it behind as quickly as possible, but Vander has retreated to the corner of the room where he collapses over an odd, lumpy pile of blankets and begins sobbing.

"Vander," I cry, flying to his side. "How badly are you hurt? We can get you whatever help you need." I tug at him, but he pulls away from my grasp. I drop to my knees and speak softly, trying to break through whatever pain and terror he's still battling. "It's okay, Vander. It's over. Ember's gone. We can go home now," I assure him.

"It's too late," he sobs. "I'm too late!"

I pull him away from the mass his torso is draped

across and gasp. It's not just blankets as I'd assumed. "Van," I whisper.

Honestly, if it weren't for Vander's reaction I might not have recognized the unconscious boy buried beneath layers of dusty, ragged blankets. His face is swollen and purpled, with streaks of blood running from his hairline to his neck. I press my fingers gently to his throat and feel the *thrum thrum* of his pulse, though it's thready and weak.

"He's alive, Vander," I say. "We can get him help."

Vander turns to me as though he's coming out of a terrible trance and only just noticed that I'm here at all. He nods, looking like he's teetering at the edge of a very high precipice, and I know he's about as close to tumbling into insanity as possible. But he can still be saved, and so can Van.

Together we hoist Van up and begin maneuvering him out the door. Soon we're surrounded by Enforcers. I think they're about to stop us, but then they grab Van by the arms and legs and help us carry him from the building.

Outside, the world has completely transformed. Dusk is setting in, and in the fading light, the lack of the ever-present orange glow of the Wall of Fire assures me that this isn't a trick or an illusion. But it's not just the Wall of Fire—all the torches are out, all The City's lights have gone dark.

Safe Dome Ten is no more.

I take only the briefest moment to breathe in the

unfiltered air and smile at the open sky, and then we're moving again. We have to get Van to the Medical Center.

The reaction of the people we pass on the streets ranges from fear to disbelief to exultant joy. People yell and cheer, and I'm not entirely sure what to expect. It's so loud that the hoverplanes are right on top of us before I even notice their approach.

I wonder how they knew to come and why, exactly, they're here.

"The City Center!" I yell over the commotion.

"Huh?" asks Vander.

"That's where a plane can set down," I cry. "We should go there."

He nods, and we change directions.

I was right, and the smallest of the hoverplanes touches down just moments later, right in the place where weeks ago every seventeen-year-old in the Flame gathered to begin a procession to the Burning.

The instant the hoverplane makes contact with the ground, the door slides open and the streets of The City are flooded with men and women wearing the blue-and-black uniforms of the SDRT led by General Rockshire. Before we know it, Van has been whisked out of our grasp and is on his way to the Hospital Wing with Vander trailing nervously after.

I step back, just trying to stay out of the way. I turn my back on the plane and look out on what's left of The City. Without the dancing light of the Wall of Fire, the place feels lifeless and hollow. I wonder if anyone will want to stay here, or if everyone will opt to be relocated to Blue Haven, or one of the other cities I'm told exists now. And I wonder—

Strong arms grab me from behind and spin me around.

"Emery!" Eason cries, pulling me to his chest.

I can hardly breathe, he holds me so tight, and yet it isn't tight enough. I wrap my arms around him and hold on as though he's my lifeline, pulling me back to safety from an endless sea of impossible challenges.

"Eason," I whisper, and it's in this moment that I really know I've succeeded.

He pulls back just enough so he can see me, and there are tears streaming down his cheeks. "Don't you ever leave me like that again," he cries with startling intensity.

"I won't," I promise, tears running down my own face, the taste of salt filling my mouth as I try to speak. "I'm so sorry. I didn't want to, but I had to," I say, begging him to understand. "I had to."

"I know," he whispers in my ear. His lips brush against my cheeks, my hair, my eyes, anywhere they can reach. "I know," he whispers again, then pulls my chin up to gaze into my eyes. "But don't ever do it again."

"I promise!"

We cling to each other, and all the chaos around us fades to a meaningless drone in the background.

And then people begin screaming, ripping us from the perfect little world encompassing only the two of us and dumping us back into reality. We turn to see over a dozen torches approaching from the direction of the Smoke. They're being carried by hideous creatures—withered men and women—Roamers.

People from The City back away in fright while Enforcers and members of the SDRT form a line, blasters pointed to hold them back.

"No," Eason cries, but no one hears over the tumult.

"Hold your fire!" a much louder and authoritative voice carries over the din as General Rockshire runs in front of the line. "They aren't going to hurt us."

Without saying a word, Eason rushes to the general's side, and together they cross the open expanse that separates us from the Roamers.

It's impossible to say what expression the Roamers wear as Eason and General Rockshire approach, as sagging and distorted as their faces appear, but I think it's something like hope.

Eason reaches out a hand to the first one he comes to, and they shake. Then, before I know what's happened, Eason and the Roamer embrace. And in that one gesture, it feels as though something historic has forever shifted.

The Enforcers and SDRT guards lower their blasters as they finally understand there's no threat here. Then the Roamers come forward, offering their torches and spreading light through the darkened city streets. Most people still keep their distance, but they don't run or scream. Children look on with curiosity, but they don't cry.

CHAPTER 25

When Eason returns to me, General Rockshire is at his side. Perhaps the biggest surprise of the night is seeing the honest-to-goodness smile on General Rockshire's face.

"You did it," he says. "But now we need to get you out of here. It's going to be a long process moving all of these people." He takes off toward the hoverplane, and Eason and I scurry along to keep up.

"How did you know to come?" I ask as we climb the steps into the familiar yellow launch room.

"When a certain transport plane arrived at Base Camp short two passengers, I started to investigate," he explains. "It took me a while to track down anyone who could tell me why you and Vander might have been heading back to Ten, but finally Aiken told me the whole story."

"And what about Elben?" I ask.

"By the time I learned what was happening, he'd taken the empty plane and left with the robot," says General Rockshire, stone-faced once again. "But don't worry. There's really nowhere for him to run."

* * *

The next day, the crowd that has gathered at Blue Haven's landing zone has to number in the hundreds. Of course, Eason and I are here waiting for people to arrive from Ten—more have been coming in every few hours. But other planes arrive intermittently from every Safe Dome—well, except One.

It turns out that when Ember decided that she was, in fact, the threat she must protect against, she used her connection to the other computers to help them see the same thing. They all deactivated simultaneously. That included the barrier fields they controlled. In one fell swoop, the entire Safe Dome "experiment" was effectively ended. Fortunately, the results were not what the Architect had hoped for.

"Aiken," I call, finding him among the waiting mass. It's the first I've seen him since before Vander and I left yesterday.

He presses his way over to us, and takes me completely off guard when he gathers me in a hug and spins me around.

"It's nice to see you, too, Aiken," I say, laughing and a little breathless.

"She's coming!" he exclaims, the exultant joy radiating from him as though he might explode any second from pure elation.

"Mara?" I ask, stupidly, because no one else could merit this kind of reaction from Aiken.

"Yes. That's her plane now," he calls over the roar of the crowd and the plane engines, pointing up at the approaching aircraft. Unable to restrain himself, he starts pushing his way to the front.

I follow, dragging Eason along.

Members of the SDRT stand along the perimeter of the assembled crowd, making sure they stand back and allow the hoverplane enough room to set down. But as soon as the vehicle is on the ground, there's no holding back Aiken, who races forward to meet it. The door opens without delay, and a steady stream of people—all dressed in immaculate finery—begin to flow out.

"I wonder how many of them are real and how many are robots?" I say to Eason, low enough that no one else will overhear, in case that question might be considered rude if any such robot should be nearby.

He shrugs.

They all look and act so perfectly humanlike, who could tell without a scanner? But what will having hundreds—or maybe thousands—of robots in Blue Haven mean, especially when most of their human counterparts are here too?

And that has me worrying about the Architect and Mara-bot again. General Rockshire may be confident that there's no more harm they can cause, but I can't be so sure. How much information does Mara-bot have stored in her memory right now? Is it enough that Elben might be tempted to try something eventually? I shudder at the thought. Fortunately, I have little time to dwell on the dark subject.

I recognize Mara—the real Mara—instantly, and not

just by the way Aiken's face breaks into an expression of acute relief and joy nearly to the point of overwhelm. I would recognize Mara easily on my own. The girl that is suddenly clinging to Aiken as though she's been suffocating and he is the only kind of oxygen that could save her really is an exact match to the robot I've gotten to know over the last week. Everything from the way she stands with more weight on her right foot than left, to her long blond hair—so light it's almost white—that she absently pulls her fingers through, to the soft but determined cadence of her voice—the voice of Mara-bot when she was focused on a problem.

"Aiken, it's really you!" she says over and over again, as though she can hardly believe it's true. "I'll probably have nightmares for the rest of my life that you've transformed into that awful robot clone I've had to pretend to love since you left."

"Is it here?" Aiken asks. I can't tell from the tone of his voice if he's merely curious to see his double or means to do it harm.

"Oh, no," Mara replies in surprise. "Didn't you hear?"

"Hear what?" I ask, unable to keep myself from interrupting their moment. But if there is news about the robots, I want to hear it.

They turn to me as though they've just suddenly realized they aren't completely alone in the universe. I understand the feeling.

"Mara, this is Emery," Aiken introduces me. "And this is Eason," he adds, but Mara is already embracing me.

"Thank you, Emery!" she says. "I owe you everything. We all do."

The gratitude carries a gravity that feels far too heavy, stifling, crushing. "It wasn't just me," I assure her. Several mouths open to reply to that comment, so I rush on before they can. I don't want to talk about me. "What were you saying about the robots?"

"Oh, right," says Mara. "When the main computer shut down, so did all of the robots."

"What?" we all mutter in astonishment.

"Yes. It turns out they were more closely tied to the computer than anyone knew. They couldn't survive without it. That was our first clue that something had happened, when people all over Sanctuary suddenly just became statues."

"And the Mara robot would be gone too, then," I surmise, hopeful.

"I can't see why not," Mara confirms.

I feel an invisible weight crumble and fall from me as I'm finally set free from the very last fear I've harbored.

"There's someone else who's been anxious to see you," Aiken tells Mara.

"Who?"

"Come on," he coaxes.

"Do you mind?" Mara asks us.

"Go right ahead," I assure her. They both turn, hand in hand, and head toward the city. I know where Aiken is taking her. Mara's Dad has been a robot for quite some time—her real father has been here, in Blue Haven, praying for the day they would be reunited.

Eason and I gaze up at the brilliant blue sky as yet another hoverplane descends. And then people we recognize begin to disembark. We meander through the crowd as members of the SDRT begin organizing the newcomers into groups and explaining what has happened, and what people's options are now. I can tell from the faces we pass that most of them aren't used to having options, and it's going to take some getting used to. But I have confidence they'll get the hang of it.

"Wait, let me get this straight," a guy is saying as we pass. "There's not going to be another round of the Burning?" I look over to see Jasper—the boy assigned to take the vacancy Eason left as Burn Master. He sounds genuinely disappointed.

"Of course not. Don't be stupid," chides Keya, who stands next to him.

"Keya!" I cry.

"Emery! Eason!"

We all embrace.

"I tried to make it out," she says, "but the tunnels were blocked by a barrier field."

So Vander must not have been mistaken about encountering a barrier field on our way into The City. Ember must have removed it because she wanted one more chance to figure out the girl who kept on baffling her. Maybe she'd been monitoring the Smoke and Ash, watching us approach for hours and hoping like a spider to ensnare us in her web.

"I'm so sorry," I say.

"But they never found me," she says with a wink. "It all worked out in the end. Who knew the impossible could happen so many times?"

I laugh. "I certainly didn't," I mutter. "I'm just too stubborn to not try anyway."

"That's because you're amazing," says Eason with a look of adoration.

"No," I contradict. "I'm just human."

EPILOGUE

The street is littered with white blossoms as the trees shed in the shifting season—not something I've ever experienced before. It's disorienting to realize that I've lived in Blue Haven for nearly half a year already. It feels simultaneously as though I've just arrived and as though I've never lived anywhere else. I think it has a lot to do with how different life is here from everything I've ever known. The two worlds—The City and Blue Haven—don't feel as though they can coexist. One or the other must be just a dream—or nightmare—not real.

I rub my forearm in the place where the Blue Haven city interface used to be. After the truth about the Safe Domes became public, no one wanted to be implanted with anything anymore. They were all removed and replaced with wrist bands that Mara helped to design. We can still communicate and do everything we need to, but we can also remove them whenever we choose.

Once people started investigating, it turned out Toren was correct, and the computer that ran the new cities wasn't nearly as impartial as everyone had been led to believe. Besides, no one wants anything that the Architect created, so it's in the process of being dismantled.

We're holding elections for city leaders, and my vote will be for Keaton, who has taken on a major role in helping to organize the city in the aftermath of all of the confusion and chaos.

A lot of people wanted General Rockshire to take on a bigger role in Blue Haven, but he's dedicated himself to a new rescue mission to find and help every Roamer that's left alive, now that we know they no longer carry the Withers. He won't say who, but I get the distinct impression that someone General Rockshire cared for very much is a Roamer now. I hope he finds them.

Doctor Gill has been working on several procedures and medications that can help to reverse a lot of the physical damage done by the disease. In fact, when I saw Gar and his parents yesterday, I almost walked right past the whole lot of them without realizing they weren't just any other healthy, happy family here in Blue Haven.

My days here have taken on a sweet and simple rhythm, gliding effortlessly along. Each morning I have breakfast with Whyle and my parents. I introduce them to new foods, and they share the favorites they remember from their childhood—before the Safe Dome. I walk Whyle to school and hug him goodbye. Then I go to work.

It took me months to decide on a job, and I still don't know if this is really where I want to stay, but for now I work with Integration Services, helping all the people coming out of the Safe Domes adjust to their new lives—

lives that can be anything they choose. It's funny how I used to think I didn't like talking to people. It turns out I love talking to people when they haven't been broken down until they hardly know what it means to be a person. I love seeing the spark of life come back to people's eyes when they understand that they're finally, truly free to live.

I approach the door to the café where Eason and I meet each day for lunch. Toren is there in his usual spot outside, handing out papers. I guess no one should be surprised that he chose to be an investigative reporter here in Blue Haven. And after all that he uncovered, people listen when he has something to say.

"How's Blue Haven fairing today?" I ask as I pass him.

"The outlook is good," he says with a smile. "But don't you worry, I'll always be watching."

"That's why I can sleep at night," I assure him with a smile.

The large glass doors to the café slide open and I enter the warm, familiar space, breathing in the scent of delicious food and endless possibilities.

Vander and Kamella are here too, sharing a table with Van and Jessamine. I'm told Vander kissed Kamella the first moment he saw her upon his return to Blue Haven. But if not, I've certainly seen him kiss her plenty since then, so I guess I can be very persuasive. Perhaps later I'll try my hand as a relationship counselor—but probably not.

Aiken and Mara—the real Mara—are just a few tables

away holding hands. They smile and wave as I enter, and Mara runs her fingers nervously through her light blond hair, just the way her robot replica always did. It's still so uncanny how similar the two Maras are, except that the real Mara isn't nearly as emotional as the robot Mara, with her jumbled programming.

Eason already has my lunch waiting for me at our usual table. It appears he's decided my usual sandwich isn't good enough for lunch today, and has replaced it with steak, potatoes, a salad, and chocolate pudding.

"Eason, how will I ever eat all of this?" I ask.

He shrugs. "I just thought today called for something special."

I take a few bites, and it is delicious. Then I notice more people I recognize: Eason's parents, Ty, Shawny with her husband and kids, Keya, Petra and Liam holding hands—when did that happen?—and even Mieka.

"Why are so many people we know here right now?" I ask, suspicious. "And why do they keep glancing over at us?" The café door opens. "And why did my family just walk in?"

Eason grimaces. "I might have mentioned something to them, but I didn't tell them to come."

"Mentioned what?"

He stands and comes around the table. At my side, he drops to one knee and takes my hand. "I left everything I cared about to join the Burning and try to save the world. I didn't know it at the time, but I was saving it all for you. And in the end, you're the one who saved me. You saved my life, and you gave me a reason to live it."

I'm stunned and speechless as every eye in the café rests on the two of us.

"Emery Kennish, I never want to be apart from you ever again. You are all I want and all I will ever want. Will you marry me?"

And before I know it, I'm down on the floor kneeling next to Eason and hugging him and laughing and crying.

"Yes," I whisper.

"What was that?" Vander calls out.

"Yes!" I cry out like a song. "A hundred million billion times, yes."

I cling to him as the room erupts into cheers. In this moment, it feels like nothing can ever be wrong with the world again, and I marvel at the thought that perhaps happy endings aren't just the things of Whyle's bedtime stories. Maybe it is possible that in the end the girl gets her prince, the kingdom is saved, the villain vanquished, and everyone lives happily ever after.

But I realize instantly that such a picture isn't quite right because no one can assure happy endings for anyone else. People like Elben try to force everyone into their neat little box of what they believe it means to be happy, safe, good, successful, or any number of other noble things—and it always turns disastrous.

No, what we've really been granted here—fought for and won—is the freedom to make our own happily-ever-afters. To wake up and strive for it each day; to let the meaning of "happily ever after" flow and shift with us.

That's the real prize worth fighting for: ownership of your own story's ending.

Read More…

SANCTUARY (FREE ebook)
Read Mara and Aiken's backstory in this Wall of Fire Companion Novella

Tech-savvy and independent, Mara has never felt like she belongs in the perfect utopia of Sanctuary. When the opportunity arises to leave and explore the treacherous, unknown world beyond, she volunteers. But in training she discovers that success could be the ultimate failure.

Download the FREE ebook
MelanieTays.com/book/sanctuary

ABOUT THE AUTHOR

Melanie Tays is an author of young adult, speculative fiction. She loves stories with twists you don't see coming, intriguing questions, and satisfying answers. She spends her days imagining how the world could be different and then takes readers along for a surprising and exciting ride.

Melanie lives in Arizona with her husband, Chris, and two brilliant daughters who keep life interesting.

Learn more about her and her latest books at MelanieTays.com.

Made in the USA
Columbia, SC
28 September 2020